© 2015 Disney. All rights reserved.

Scholastic Children's Books
Euston House,
24 Eversholt Street,
London NW1 1DB, UK

A division of Scholastic Ltd
London ~ New York ~ Toronto ~ Sydney ~ Auckland
Mexico City ~ New Delhi ~ Hong Kong

Published in the UK by Scholastic Ltd, 2015

Original project developed by Disney Publishing with the contribution of Barbara
Baraldi, Paola Barbato, Micol Beltramini and Diana Tomatozombie

Cover illustration layout and clean-up: Alberto Zanon
Cover illustration colour: Massimo Rocca

ISBN 978 14071 5800 6

Printed and bound by CPI Group (UK) Ltd, Croydon, CR0 4YY

2 4 6 8 10 9 7 5 3 1

Papers used by Scholastic Children's Books are
made from woods grown in sustainable forests.

www.scholastic.co.uk

Disney

real life
Who's That Boy?

Scarlett Blake

SCHOLASTIC

Every day, hundreds of students from all over the world crowd the hallways of London International High School in Marylebone, one of the city's most prestigious schools. Some are best friends; others barely know each other; a few are sworn enemies. But they all have something in common: a profile on the school's social network, Real Life.

Real Life is where everything happens, where photos and comments are posted and taken down, where friendships are made, played out and broken. Popularity is crucial. Virtual fame is everything.

If you're not on Real Life, you don't exist.

'You're in trouble!'

It was Friday afternoon and the hallways of London International High School were buzzing. Snatches of laughter and gossip filled the air as students grabbed their books and moved off in different directions to their classrooms. But in the head teacher's office there was silence. You could have cut the atmosphere with a knife.

Three very different students stood in a line before the head. Amber Lee Thompson, the undisputed queen bee of the school, folded her arms sulkily across her chest. Everything about Amber seemed to declare her contempt for the situation, from her defiant green eyes to the shock of auburn hair slanting moodily across her forehead.

This is a complete waste of time, she thought. *Get me out of here now.*

She had already clashed with Mrs Barnes once today and was still glowing with resentment. The most popular girl in the school was not used to being overruled.

Standing next to Amber was Andrea Tanaka, looking oddly dishevelled. Andrea's shirt was creased and her dark hair – usually so shiny and neat – was unbrushed. Her large brown eyes were full of concern as she waited to hear what Mrs Barnes had to say – and how it would affect her studies.

How much longer is she going to keep us here? she wondered. Andrea could just about deal with the injustice of being summoned to the head teacher's office, but only if it didn't interfere with her grades. She had to remain a top student if she was going to be accepted at Yale summer school in America.

'You three are in trouble!' Mrs Barnes said finally, glaring at them from under her stiff helmet of hair.

At the end of the row next to Andrea, Alice Keats gasped softly. Her shoulders tensed and her hands flew to her mouth. *No, no, this is so unfair*, she thought, her mind whirring with panic. Loose strands of blonde hair fell over her frightened face.

'Each of you has broken a very serious rule,' Mrs Barnes continued.

Yawn, thought Amber. *Wake me up when the lecture is over!*

'And the London International High School does not tolerate rule breaking,' she went on. 'Therefore, I am going to make an example of all three of you.' She paused.

I don't deserve this, thought Andrea. *I should be getting a medal, not being punished.*

Alice hung her head in shame, wishing the earth would swallow her up.

How could I have been so stupid? she fretted. *What will my parents say when they find out?*

Amber spoke first. 'What happened wasn't my fault, Mrs Barnes, and you know it.'

Mrs Barnes pursed her lips. 'I'm not here to assign blame, but to punish you and your friends.'

Amber made a face. 'They're not my friends,' she protested. *Ugh*, she thought, without even a sideways glance at Andrea or Alice.

'In that case, it is an even more fitting punishment, as you will be spending three afternoons closeted together, reorganizing the library.'

Was that all? Amber grinned; she could probably get the others to do all the hard work while she chatted and messaged her friends on Real Life. Meanwhile, Andrea couldn't see how organizing books could be classed as a punishment, especially as the library was one of her favourite places. Alice was just thankful that she hadn't been suspended.

Mrs Barnes frowned. 'You're smiling?' she said. 'Don't celebrate yet. I will be asking the librarian to confiscate your mobiles for the duration of the punishment.'

Alice's blue eyes grew wide. 'We won't be able to access Real Life?'

'Or check our profiles?' Andrea asked, thinking of her study notes.

'No social life for three afternoons?' Amber said in disbelief.

A stunned silence followed.

The head regarded them with satisfaction. 'That is correct,' she said, picking a piece of fluff off her tweed suit. 'Now get back to your lessons.'

Ten minutes later, in the ground-floor bathroom – also known as Amber's 'office' – Amber's faithful followers, Lynn and Jess, were hovering around her attentively. The school queen bee was rarely seen without her sidekicks. Neither dark, sultry Lynn nor awkward, mousey Jess looked anything like their red-haired leader – and they had none of her natural charm. But they dressed like her, acted like her and laughed at all her jokes.

Right then, Amber wasn't smiling, though. 'What am I going to do?' she said, staring at her phone. 'Lynn, Jess, you've got to help me!'

'How?' Jess asked helplessly.

Lynn's face lit up. 'I know! If you give me your Real Life password, I can post comments on your profile for you while you're in detention.'

Jess looked pained. 'Take responsibility for replacing the star of Real Life? Yeesh!'

'No way!' Amber snapped. 'I don't want to come out of detention to find I'm the most unpopular girl in the school. Think of something else. This is serious.'

Lynn looked crestfallen. 'I'm just trying—'

'Hey,' Amber interrupted, 'if I write a list of comments now, do you think I can make Real Life post them while I'm in the library?'

Lynn and Jess watched eagerly as she tapped her keypad.

A message appeared on her phone.

SYSTEM ERROR
Automatic post not available

Amber stamped her feet in fury.

Andrea went looking for Jay. She found him on a bench in the courtyard, reading an old superhero comic. With his square glasses, ruffled hair and baggy retro T-shirt, he looked like your average comic-book nerd. But he was so much more than that – especially to her. He was her best friend and had been since the day they had met.

Jay looked really happy to see her. Then he frowned. 'What's wrong?' he asked.

She recounted the events of her day. 'It's so unfair. I did nothing wrong!' she burst out.

'You call pouring mayonnaise on someone's head "nothing"?' he asked, amazed.

Andrea pouted. 'You're supposed to be on my side!' she complained. 'Anyway, he deserved it.'

Jay took off his glasses and smiled at her. 'Whatever you say.'

'And now I've got a serious problem,' Andrea said. 'All my school notes are on my Real Life profile. What am I going to do?'

Jay chuckled. 'Try writing them on paper next time?'

Alice found her brother, Daniel, intently practising kick-ups alone on the football pitch. 'Well done on getting caught in the boys' changing rooms,' he said, as he floated the ball onto his chest. 'Dad will be proud.'

'You're not going to tell him, are you?' Alice asked.

Daniel turned away and took a shot at goal. 'Come on, he's the school volleyball coach. You really think he's not going to find out?'

'But you'll help me, won't you?'

Alice had a fleeting image of Daniel, tall, blonde and athletic, dressed as an ancient warrior, threatening to attack the head teacher if she didn't withdraw her punishment. She had always looked up to her older brother. He'd been her hero since they were little.

'Not this time, little sis,' he said firmly. 'You need to learn to solve your own problems.'

Her blue eyes welled up as he walked away, football in hand, abandoning her to her fate. She had come looking for support, but Daniel wasn't going to be her champion any more. How was she going to get by without him?

Amber scowled when she saw the towering piles of books stacked up against the windows. They were blocking out the daylight, making the library seem gloomier than ever.

'These were all returned after the last school holidays,' explained Rachel, the librarian. 'I doubt any of them has been read – but now they all have to be put back in their place. It's quite a job, so I suggest you get to work.'

'What about him?' Andrea was pointing at a boy slumped in a chair with his head resting on the table, gently snoring.

Rachel nodded absently. 'Dylan can help as well,' she said, making no attempt to wake him up. Dylan Simmons was the world's worst student. Was he ever out of detention?

Amber found a chair and sat down with a sigh of

frustration. She felt lost without her phone, which was now locked in Rachel's desk. *This totally sucks*, she thought. Cut off from reality, she felt trapped in a murky void of half-existence. It was like a really boring nightmare. For the thousandth time that day she cursed Edward Bradford-Taylor. This was all his fault.

She ran her fingers through her cloud of auburn hair. The school's social network was her life support system and she knew exactly how to work it – when to post, when to hang back and how to build anticipation for her next wittily barbed comment. Being the most popular girl in school meant being visible online, so she was terrified of being disconnected. People would forget her; they'd find a new queen bee.

'Amber who?' they'd say, wrinkling their eyebrows. 'Oh, her.'

It could be worse, Andrea decided, as she sized up the task ahead. OK, she wouldn't get to read any of the books, but a part of her enjoyed bringing order to chaos. Or that's what she told herself as she tried not to think about the fact that she couldn't get hold of her class notes without access to Real Life. She was also trying to forget the look of total shock on Jay's face when she told him about what she'd done in the school cafeteria. Perhaps it hadn't been such a good idea, after all. As her mind began to whir out of control, she sensed that the only way to calm down would be to focus on the afternoon's assignment. *Books. Organize. Now.*

Alice was dreading the moment she would have to face her parents. It was so unfair. Especially as the whole school was laughing at her, after one of the basketball team had taken a photo of her cringing in the boys' changing rooms and posted it on Real Life, in a gallery specially reserved for her, #embarrassingmoments. Worst of all, that boy just happened to be James, the boy she had been secretly crazy about – and maybe still was. Only, what was the point? He had laughed the loudest. She should just forget him.

'No slacking, now,' Rachel said as she left the library. 'Don't forget, Mrs Barnes will be coming in to check on you.'

Amber groaned. 'I really don't deserve this!'

What are you doing here?

Andrea picked up a thick volume of poetry. 'We'd better get started.'

Alice jumped to her feet, her long hair flying. 'Let's go!' she said. 'If we work together, we'll get it done quicker.'

'Whoa!' Amber raised a hand in protest. 'Don't even think about telling me what to do. I'm not on your team, OK?'

Alice wilted, even though it was no real surprise that Amber wanted nothing to do with her. Her whole life seemed to be linked by a series of disasters and misunderstandings. The only place she really shone was on the volleyball court. The rest of the time she just felt awkward, lanky and self-conscious. Oh, and unpopular, too.

'If you're not planning to help, at least wake Dylan up,' Andrea said.

Amber glanced over at Dylan. 'No, leave him,' she said. 'I'd rather help than have him around.' For some inexplicable reason he was her best friend Meg's boyfriend, but she avoided having to deal with him if she could.

'Fine. Take this, then.' Andrea handed her a book.

'What is it?' Amber scanned the cover and hurled it at Alice. 'Ugh, get that away from me.'

Alice fumbled for it and let the big pile of books she was holding go crashing to the floor. 'You're a walking disaster zone, Keats!' Amber scoffed. 'You're lucky I can't post on Real Life, because that would be yet another embarrassing moment photo to add to all the rest.'

Andrea knelt down to help Alice clear up the mess. She picked up the book Amber had flung away. 'What's your problem with *Romeo and Juliet*?'

'It's boring,' Amber said, not meeting her eye.

'It's also going to be the end-of-year show. Edward Bradford-Taylor's directing,' Alice added.

'So?' said Andrea. 'Hey, isn't Edward your boyfriend?' she asked Amber.

'I dumped him, a week ago,' Amber said dismissively. 'You must be the last person in the school to know, Tanaka. Everyone was talking about it on Real Life.'

Andrea bristled. 'Oh, forgive me if I have better things to do than keep up with your gossip. So you won't be Juliet, is that the problem?'

'Amber was supposed to direct this year's show,' Alice said. 'Almost everybody voted for her.'

'It wasn't some dullsville ancient tragedy, either,' Amber

burst out, unable to contain herself. 'My idea for a rock opera crushed *Romeo and Juliet*; it crushed everything. Today was going to be my perfect day. I got dressed up like a diva, ready to put my heartbreak behind me and—'

Andrea interrupted her. 'Heartbreak? Didn't you say *you* dumped Edward?'

Amber glared at her. 'Look, I dumped him, but he still broke my heart – I thought he was my prince . . . he wasn't.' She toyed with her hair again. Despite his awesome good looks and hero status, Edward wasn't actually very nice.

'I was all set to get my revenge today,' she went on, 'then Mrs Barnes announced that my musical *Rock Lady* "was not a suitable vehicle to represent the drama class of LIHS". She's totally out of touch! I couldn't believe it – everybody else was behind it. And *Romeo and Juliet*? It's so unoriginal. Somehow he must have persuaded her to do it, I just know it.'

She recalled her argument with Edward after Mrs Barnes broke the news. He'd been triumphant and she was so angry that the whole thing had escalated into a slanging match. It still stung when she remembered that Edward had told her, in front of the entire drama class, that kissing her was like kissing a snail. How could he be so cruel?

Andrea handed her another book. 'So how did you end up here? What did you do?'

Amber hung her head. 'I downloaded a photo of a guy taking a dog for a walk, replaced the faces and posted it on Real Life.'

'Oh no,' Andrea said softly.

'Five minutes later I deleted it, but someone had already sent it to Mrs Barnes.'

'Don't tell me the picture showed Edward walking Mrs Barnes like a dog on a leash?'

'Yup.'

'That's bad.'

Amber bit her lip. 'Well, I was angry!'

'He dumped you, didn't he?' Andrea said.

'What?'

'Edward dumped you.'

'That's ridiculous,' Amber snapped. 'Take it back!'

'That's why you're so bitter. It's not just the show.'

Amber swiped at the books in Andrea's hands. 'I said, take it back. Now!'

'Cut it out!' Andrea yelped. 'You think you're the only one with boy problems?'

They locked eyes, challenging each other to go further. Then, sensing she might not win this particular battle, Amber changed the subject. 'So, what did you do to end up here, Miss Study Boots? I'm guessing you're not being punished for doing too much homework.'

'Don't you get it?' Andrea retorted. 'It's a boy's fault I'm here too. . .'

'Go on,' Amber said, intrigued despite herself. Andrea and a guy? How unexpected.

Andrea looked at the floor. 'I thought I'd found the perfect boy.'

Amber rolled her eyes. 'Let me guess, a soulmate and study buddy rolled into one?'

Andrea sighed. Amber had that right. Her heart had skipped for joy as Jordan Cross told her about his passion for photography, biology, maths and chemistry. She had never been particularly interested in boys – it wasn't that she hadn't thought about them, but her schoolwork had always been more important. Then along came Jordan, who loved to study, aced his grades and was a million times better looking than any of the other academic students she knew. *Marry me!* she'd thought, her mind racing.

She told them how she had offered to help him catch up in history and literature. She helped a lot of students in her class, but this would be different, she was sure. Jordan had happily accepted and she hadn't been able to stop smiling at the thought of studying together. She didn't realize how badly she had misjudged the situation until he got out his phone and texted his dad to tell him to buy him a motorbike, because he was sure to get good grades now that he'd found his own little nerd to do his homework for him.

'What is it?' he'd asked, laughing nastily when he saw the look of disappointment on her face. 'Don't tell me you thought I wanted to go out with you?'

Andrea hesitated as she came to the last part of the story. 'And then he asked me to pass him some mayonnaise and I guess something came over me, because I dumped the entire pot on his head. . . I guess I got carried away. . .'

'Pure genius! I love it!' Amber squealed, gleefully throwing her arms around her.

Andrea pushed her away. 'Don't,' she said. 'We're not friends. I'm just telling you why I'm here.'

'You're right, what was I thinking?' Amber said, giving Andrea a cool, appraising look. 'I'd never hang out with someone as badly dressed as you.'

'Good. That's why I dress this way,' Andrea said, although she was secretly smarting at Amber's words. 'To keep people like you at a distance!'

Amber took some gloss and a hand mirror out of her schoolbag. 'Whatever,' she said, shining her lips.

Alice coughed. 'It's weird that we're all here because of a boy, isn't it?' she said.

'We all know what happened to you, Keats,' Andrea said.

'Did you really think you wouldn't get caught spying on James in the boys' changing rooms?' Amber asked. 'The photos were all over Real Life.'

'You think everything you see on Real Life is true? It's not.'

'Photos don't lie.'

'People do, though,' Alice said. 'It's all James's fault. He's worse than Edward and Jordan put together.'

'Why? Because he's got a sense of humour?' Amber asked.

Alice sighed. 'You think you're the only ones to be let down by a boy?'

'We're listening,' Amber said, hand on hip.

Alice took a deep breath. 'So, I went to meet my brother outside the changing rooms to get back a maths book I'd lent him. But he wasn't there – and when I messaged him, he told me to go in and get it out of his backpack.'

She clenched her fists as she remembered the part her brother, Daniel, had played in her downfall.

ALICE KEATS

Go into the boys' changing rooms?

Are you crazy?

DANIEL KEATS

Yes, if you need it now.

ALICE KEATS

But you were supposed to meet

me and give it to me!

DANIEL KEATS

I'm at football practice. Sort it out
yourself, sis.

Alice winced at the memory as she told them how, as soon as she'd found the maths book in Daniel's locker, the changing-room doors opened and the basketball team piled in, leaving her hiding in the showers. When she decided to try to make her escape, she ran right into James, tripped on a PE kit and fell flat on her face. He took a picture of her sprawled on the ground, and posted it on Real Life: #embarrassingmoments #DisasterKeatsstrikesagain.

'You see?' she said indignantly to Amber and Andrea. 'I wasn't spying. It was a total mistake.'

Amber doubled over laughing. 'You're a disaster magnet, Keats. Has it ever occurred to you that you could make things so much easier for yourself by not trying so hard?'

Alice's lip began to tremble. 'Thanks for the support,' she mumbled.

Andrea hid her smile and put a comforting hand on Alice's shoulder. 'Look on the positive side,' she said. 'At least you know what James is really like now. Don't waste another thought on him.'

'You're right,' Alice said, on the verge of tears. 'But I can't help it. How could he be so mean? Fine, he doesn't like me, but to make fun of me like that. . .'

'What's going on here?' boomed a familiar voice.

The three girls turned to see the head teacher standing in the doorway with a face like thunder.

'You're not helping yourselves by standing around chatting,' she said sternly. 'I wouldn't want to have to add another detention to the three you already have.'

They looked at each other in dismay and tried to look busy as she swept out of the room. Another detention would really suck.

Who's that boy?

Andrea prodded Dylan. 'Wake up and start helping! You're not in bed, you're in detention.'

'Hey, get your hands off my boyfriend!' someone yelled. Andrea whipped round. A girl with fierce brown eyes was looking daggers at her. Dressed head to toe in rock-chick chic, her dip-dyed hair was styled into punky angles.

'Megan!' cried Amber, rushing forward to hug her. 'I couldn't even message you.'

Megan hugged her back. 'Lynn and Jess told me everything – and Mum said I could come in and see you for a couple of minutes.'

I guess it helps to be the librarian's daughter, Andrea thought.

Dylan sat up, his brown eyes still half-closed. 'You're late,' he said sulkily.

Megan leaned into him and kissed his cheek. 'Sorry, babe.' She turned back to Amber. 'Bad day, huh?'

Amber let her guard drop as she poured out her troubles to her best friend. 'First, I didn't get the show,' she complained, 'then Real Life was taken away from me – and it's all that jerk Edward's fault. I hate him!'

Megan hugged her friend again. 'What did I tell you? Edward's an idiot. He never really loved you.'

Amber winced. 'I know, you were right, I should have listened, but...' She shrugged and looked at Dylan. 'Sometimes you just fall for the wrong person, I guess.'

'We'll teach Edward a lesson,' Megan declared.

Amber laughed. 'Revenge? Payback? I like your style – but how?'

Dylan put his arm round Megan. 'Time to go,' he drawled.

Amber's face fell. 'Already?'

'Sorry, darling, we've got band practice. The Sad Cats can't wait!' Megan said.

'But Dylan can't go anywhere,' Alice told Megan.

Dylan spun around. 'You gonna tell Mrs Barnes on me?' he hissed.

Andrea stepped in. 'No one's going to tell on anyone,' she assured him.

Dylan turned back to Megan and they headed for the door. 'We'll see, won't we?' he muttered as they left.

Andrea folded her arms in disapproval as she watched them go. 'What a couple of loons.'

'Hey, don't say things like that about my best friend!' Amber protested.

People might criticize Amber, Alice thought. But no one could ever accuse her of being disloyal.

'I'm not surprised she's your best friend,' Andrea frowned. 'You have the same dumb taste in boys.'

Amber raised her perfectly shaped eyebrows. 'That's funny, coming from a loser like you,' she said scornfully. 'You think you're better than us? At least Megan has a boyfriend! Meanwhile, you're waiting around for the perfect boy to come along and fall in love with your oh-so-brilliant brain. Well, it won't happen. One, the perfect boy doesn't exist; two, even if he did, he wouldn't look at you! Face it, Tanaka, you're going to be alone with your precious books and grades for ever.'

Andrea turned her back on Amber and walked away, head lowered.

'Don't tell me you're going to start crying,' Amber said.

Andrea shrugged.

'The perfect boy has to be out there somewhere,' Alice murmured.

'Forget it, Keats,' Amber said. 'That guy you dream about before you go to sleep? You'll never, ever meet him.'

Alice sighed. 'But think how cool it would be if we could create him ourselves.'

She heard a soft exclamation. Andrea was walking towards the library computer. 'What are you doing?'

Alice asked, as the computer screen lit up. Andrea didn't reply.

Intrigued, Amber and Alice watched her as she pulled up the Real Life home page. Amber's green eyes grew wider. 'Go to my profile!' she blurted out, desperate to see what was happening in her absence.

'I want to see mine too!' Alice said.

Andrea shook her head. 'If we log in to our profiles, we'll get caught.'

'So why are you opening Real Life?'

'I'm making a new profile.'

'Whose?'

Andrea smiled. 'The perfect boy's, of course.'

She dragged an image into the photo box. It was a sketch she'd done of her ideal boyfriend, ages ago. She'd uploaded it to an online drawing contest, under a fake name. Not that she was going to tell the others that. Andrea gazed at him for a moment. He was practically perfect – serious, slightly moody, but in a dreamy, gorgeous way.

'Who's he?' Amber asked, more interested than she would have liked to admit. It was just a drawing, but she liked his eyes – they were deep and mysterious, with a roguish glint.

'No one,' lied Andrea. 'It's just a picture I found.'

'He's cute!' Alice said, wondering what star sign he was.

'Super-cute,' agreed Amber. 'Let me guess, Tanaka, he loves to study?'

Andrea nodded as she filled in the empty profile boxes. Under 'Likes' she wrote: Studying – history, literature, chemistry, biology, maths and astronomy. Under 'Dislikes' she wrote: Photography, Jordan Cross and mayonnaise.

If he existed, this boy would be able to solve even the most difficult maths equation in the blink of an eye – and then he'd ask her on a date to the Royal Observatory.

'Boring!' Amber said. 'What's his name?'

'He's my perfect boy, not yours,' Andrea said. 'He hasn't got a name yet. I'm working on it.'

'Let me do it.' Amber elbowed her out of the way and sat down in front of the computer. 'How about Thomas Anderson?'

In a flash she added '*Romeo and Juliet*', 'Edward Bradford-Taylor' and 'the head teacher' to his dislikes. Her perfect boy would be romantic and smart and offer her a ride home on a white horse, Prince Charming-style.

'Prince Charming? That is so lame. You've ruined him!' Andrea objected.

'Come on, Tanaka, it's way better than Prince Maths Equation!'

'Ugh, you've got the worst taste in boys.'

Amber stood up and pointed a finger in Andrea's

face. 'You have no idea what romance means. I'd be asleep after two minutes with your boring date.'

'Ha, I'd like to see you riding along on that white horse, with your perfect hairstyle all messed up and your clothes covered in horse hair.'

As the others argued, Alice slipped into the empty chair in front of the computer and added her preferences to the profile of Thomas Anderson. He would be a Libra, her perfect Zodiac match, and he'd love *Romeo and Juliet*. Naturally he'd hate James – and he'd be sweet and protective, the kind of boy who would pull you close under his umbrella to shelter you from the rain.

'*Whaaat?*' Alice looked up to see Amber standing behind her. 'He does not like *Romeo and Juliet*! Delete it! He hates every word of that play.'

Alice jumped out of the chair and tried to get away, but instead caught her foot on the computer lead, unplugging it at both ends. In an instant, the power supply disconnected and Thomas Anderson's profile vanished.

'No!' shrieked Andrea.

'Nice move, Disaster Keats,' Amber said.

Alice scrabbled to put the cable back.

'It won't have saved the data,' Andrea said. 'Thomas Anderson no longer exists.'

'We could rewrite it?' Alice suggested.

'In your dreams,' Amber said. Glancing at the library clock, she added, 'Torture over, for today at least.' She adjusted a hair clip, slung her bag over her shoulder and strutted off. 'Bye, losers.'

Andrea put her hands in her jacket pockets. 'I guess I'll go home and study,' she said, but she didn't sound very enthusiastic.

Alice stared guiltily after Andrea as she disappeared around the corner. As usual she had ruined things. But maybe...? She ran after her. 'Wait for me! Which way do you go home?' But the hallway outside the library was empty.

Alice didn't hear the beep of the computer as she shut the door. She was totally unaware that with the cable back in it had switched itself on and rebooted by the time she had reached her bicycle.

While Amber hailed a taxi, wishing she were on the back of Edward's motorbike, a message appeared on the school library computer announcing that data recovery was 43% complete.

As Andrea sat on the bus going home, she wondered if she would ever meet a boy she really liked. Maybe Amber was right and she would always be alone.

Data recovery: 67% complete, 81% complete, 96% complete.

Alice was cycling furiously through the busy London streets, wondering if her parents already knew about her detention, when data recovery reached 100%. Thomas Anderson's profile had been reinstated, and not one of the students who had created him knew a thing about it.

Anyone passing the school library that evening would have seen a strange glow lighting up the room, shortly before a fire started. Was it just the glimmer of the flames? Or was it something else altogether?

On Monday morning, no one seemed to care that Amber was back on Real Life. All anyone cared about was that a fire that had burned down the library on Friday evening.

EDWARD BRADFORD-TAYLOR
Best Monday of the year!

JAMES COLLINS
Let's get a photo!

BILL MARTIN
I'm glad it wasn't the dining hall, ha ha ha!

MEGAN GARRITY
It happened on Friday?

So the library burned down, Amber thought. *Who cares! Why hasn't anyone noticed what I'm wearing?* Over the weekend she had picked out several sample dresses from her fashion designer mother's new collection, before choosing one that complemented her striking hair and eyes.

'Monster ankle boots!' Two girls rushed over to pay homage to her footwear.

That's better, she thought. Nobody could dispute that she was a goddess of style.

Moments later, Lynn and Jess found her. Lynn was beaming. 'No library means no detention, right?' Jess did a little jump for joy.

'As long as I don't have to spend another minute with Keats and Tanaka,' Amber said, rolling her eyes. Her sidekicks sniggered. 'And it means I'll be finished in time to go home with. . .'

She saw Edward in the hallway, looking tall and gorgeous as ever.

'Amber,' he said. 'Just the person. . . I wanted to say that I won't be able to take you home any more, because I'll be staying late at the theatre.'

'Of course,' she mumbled, looking at the floor. 'Anyway, I wouldn't. . .'

He was gone.

She kept her head down, her abundant red hair falling forward and obscuring her face as she slowly walked on.

'Everything OK?' Jess asked.

'Of course,' she said abruptly. 'Come on, let's go.'

Her phone beeped.

FRIEND REQUEST
From Thomas Anderson

'What?' She frowned as she read the message. 'Ha ha. Those losers think it's funny to play tricks on me, do they? We'll see about that.' She marched off, without a word of explanation to Lynn or Jess.

She found Andrea and Alice in one of the science rooms. 'What do you think you're doing?' she yelled. 'Do you have any idea what happens to people who mess with Amber Lee Thompson?'

Alice cowered behind Andrea. 'Calm down, Miss Popular,' Andrea said, quaking slightly. 'If this is about Thomas, we also got a friend request from him.'

'What did you say?' Amber hissed.

Andrea held up her phone to show her. 'I got one and so did Alice.'

'You expect me to believe that?'

'Go on Real Life and look for Thomas Anderson's profile.'

Amber checked her phone. 'But. . .' She looked up, astonished. 'What does it mean?'

28

'It's totally crazy – the profile we made up still exists,' Alice said.

Amber glared at Andrea. 'Existing is one thing. But sending out its own friend requests? I don't think so. Nice try, super-brain. Now delete it!'

Andrea held her hands up. 'Look, it wasn't me.'

'It wasn't either of us,' Alice added quickly.

'Who was it then?'

Andrea racked her brain for a logical answer. 'The profile was definitely deleted, I'm sure of it. Plus, the computer was destroyed in the library fire; the data would have been irretrievable… I don't know how anything could survive a double wipe-out like that.'

'Maybe, after we left, Dylan came back and rewrote everything,' Alice suggested, off the top of her head. 'Or it could have been the librarian, or the head – yes, that's it, Mrs Barnes!'

'That's the stupidest thing I've ever heard,' Amber snarled. She made for the door. 'What am I doing here? I don't even want to be seen talking to you!'

'Wait!' Andrea raced after Amber, closely followed by Alice. They bundled out into the hallway together and ran straight into the head teacher.

'Don't think I've forgotten about your punishment,' the head said, striding off down the corridor. 'But first things first – I must go and welcome our new student, Thomas Anderson.'

The girls watched her go. 'Did I just hear her say, Thomas Anderson?' Alice said.

'Not possible,' Andrea said, walking away.

'You're obsessed, Keats,' Amber sniffed.

Alice was left standing on her own. *I heard his name*, she thought. *I know I did.*

Over the next few hours, the hallways and classrooms of the London International High School buzzed with rumours about the new student. Megan bounded up to Amber as she was leaving her history class with Lynn and Jess. 'Everyone's saying he's gorgeous, and the football and basketball teams are already fighting over him,' she said. 'I wonder when we'll get to meet him. . .' Her voice trailed off. 'Not that I care, obviously. I have Dylan.'

Amber flicked her eyes skywards. 'So what's this amazing new guy's name?'

Megan shrugged.

'Do you know anything?' a couple of girls asked Alice, a few paces behind Amber and Megan.

'Why would I?'

'If he's that good at football, your brother, Daniel, will know who he is.'

In the study rooms, Jay was telling Andrea about a boy who had helped Bill Martin hack a vending machine. 'The guy must be a genius! Those machines are bust-proof,' Jay was saying. 'I'd like to meet this Thomas Anderson.'

Andrea practically jumped out of her seat.

'Back to chemistry.' Jay sighed, picking up a book. 'I need to know what to do if I get superpowers after falling into a radioactive bath.'

But Andrea was already gone.

In the girls' changing rooms, there was just one subject of conversation among the members of the volleyball team as they got changed for practice.

'He's, like, really hot!'

'He told Roxy Middlescott he's a Libra!'

'I heard that too. His birthday's 29th September.'

'He told me he wants to act in *Romeo and Juliet*.'

'You met him?'

Alice listened in disbelief. A Libra? *Romeo and Juliet*? It was too weird. It couldn't be a coincidence. But it had to be. Yet it couldn't be. The possibility was dizzying – and so was the impossibility. What was the truth? She had to find out. She left the locker room in a hurry and messaged Daniel, who immediately ticked her off for skipping volleyball practice.

ALICE KEATS
Is Thomas Anderson on your team?

DANIEL KEATS
Why do you care?

31

ALICE KEATS

This is serious, Danny. Is he with you?

DANIEL KEATS

Just tell me why you want to know.

ALICE KEATS

DAN, PLEASE!

DANIEL KEATS

He left the pitch about ten minutes ago. I think
he's going home. Why?

She raced out of the building and stood on the
steps, her heart pounding as she waited for a glimpse
of him. *I need to see him*, she thought. *Just to make sure
that it's not* my *Thomas Anderson.*

It started to rain, so she held up her book bag
for shelter. 'Where's your umbrella, Keats?' someone
called out. 'You look like a complete weirdo standing
there with a bag on your head.'

Another #embarrassingmoment? She kept on
waiting, in spite of the rain.

This is so crazy, she thought. *Of course it's not going
to be my Thomas.*

Suddenly, there was someone beside her, using his
jacket to shelter her from the rain. Hardly daring to

breathe, she turned and saw a face she recognized, although she had never seen it before.

Brown hair, straight nose, dark eyes with a hint of mischief... Her stomach flipped over. *It's the boy from the drawing*, she thought. *It's really him. And he's gorgeous.*

'You don't need an umbrella if I'm here, Alice,' he said, gently guiding her down the steps.

How does he know my name? she thought. *It's impossible. He's not real, he can't be.*

In an instant, it stopped raining. The boy lowered his jacket and moved away from her, holding her gaze, looking deep into her puzzled eyes, asking silent questions of his own. Then he smiled. It felt like the sun had just come out. She stared back at him in wonder, unable to speak or move, her whole world framed by a huge pink heart.

Andrea found Bill Martin chomping a bag of chips in the main hallway. There was tomato sauce on his goatee. 'Bill!'

'Hi, Tanaka,' he said, his cheeks bulging. He glanced at his phone screen. 'Let's see, I'm free for you tomorrow and Thursday.'

Andrea had no time for Bill's jokes. 'Stop it, I'm not here to ask you out.'

'Don't turn your back on love, Andrea!' he cried.

Resisting the impulse to be sick on the spot, she said, 'Do you know where Thomas Anderson is?'

'Anderson? Tall, handsome, intelligent, nice guy? Basically a worse version of me?'

'Yes. Him.'

Bill pointed at a door. 'Maths class. Just went in.'

Andrea ran off, her black hair flying behind her. Bill dug his hand into the bag of chips and sighed to himself. 'It's amazing how the girls at this school let all the best opportunities pass them by.'

In the maths classroom, someone was standing at the blackboard, midway through solving an equation.

Andrea's heart started to thump. 'Um, hi, you're the new student, right?'

She recognized him the moment he turned around, the way his dark eyes sparkled with intelligence, the warm-hearted expression on his handsome face. He was her perfect boy, the boy whose face she had sketched one night while she was dreaming of love and later attached to Thomas Anderson's profile. Yet how could he be? It just wasn't logical.

He wrote a few more numbers and symbols on the board and then dropped the chalk into a dish. 'I heard that Mr Austin gives extra credit to whoever solves the equations he leaves here at the end of the class.' He smiled apologetically. 'Maybe next time we can solve it together.'

As he walked past her, Andrea felt like her head was preparing to separate from her body and blast off into space. It was the weirdest sensation, a mix of confusion and total . . . what was it?

3-2-1, lift off! screamed her brain.

I'm coming too! yelled her heart.

Amber had given up looking for the new student and given up caring. She had other things on her mind. Like how much she was going to miss riding home with Edward. She loved to be seen on his motorbike and felt so alive weaving through the London streets with her arms clasped around him. Now it was over.

She heard a voice. 'Did the queen order a ride?'

Edward? Her heart leaped as she turned. *Wait, who is that?*

Up ahead she saw a boy leaning casually against a motorbike. His hair was mussed up and he was wearing black jeans and a green biker jacket. Their eyes locked. *He looks just like the guy in the drawing*, she thought idly. *Hang on, he's exactly like the guy in the drawing!*

Thomas's dark eyes glittered as he waited for Amber to answer his question. She moved closer to him – magnetized, mesmerized – and noticed an emblem gleaming on the motorcycle's petrol tank. A white horse.

She drew in a sharp breath. *It is him!* she thought. *It is Thomas Anderson*, my *Thomas Anderson. My knight in shining armour.*

*

That night in their bedrooms across London, Amber, Andrea and Alice stared wordlessly at their computers, gazing at Thomas's Real Life profile, questions whirring in their heads.

Who are you? Did we really make you up? How did we do it?

As the evening wore on, they went over and over what had happened, analysing every moment of each encounter and dreaming about the possibilities.

For Alice and Amber, confusion soon gave way to happiness. *He's just how I imagined my perfect boy*, they thought.

Only Andrea couldn't relax. There were too many unanswered questions for her scientific brain to accept.

He said everything I wanted him to say, but how did he know what I wanted him to say? Things like that don't happen in reality.

Before the end of the night, they had all sent Thomas a message asking him if they could meet up with him before school.

What if he really was the perfect boy?

Can dreams come true?

Alice woke up from a dream about Thomas with her arms tightly clasped around a pillow. She closed her eyes, willing herself to go back to sleep, but reality had already kicked in. Lying on her bed, the last fragments of the dream swirled in her head – one moment they were on the volleyball court together, the next they were alone in a quiet courtyard in Verona. She was Juliet, he was Romeo, and he was holding her close. His cheek brushed against hers, he murmured soft words in her ear. 'May your dreams come true,' he whispered, leaning in towards her. Just as their lips were about to touch...

...the dream ended.

I'm in trouble, Alice thought, sitting bolt upright. *I can't stop thinking about him. I'm mad about him, I want to go out with him and, worst of all, I want to act opposite him in the end-of-year show.*

Nobody knew about Alice's secret dream to go onstage. It was something she was almost ashamed of. But she sensed that Thomas would understand.

Her phone beeped. Thomas? Her face felt hot as she looked at the screen.

Wrong. Not Thomas.

APPOINTMENT

Team selection at 4 p.m.

Volleyball. Oh right. That was her life.

'Wake up, honey!' her mother called. 'Don't forget that today's a really important day.'

Here goes, she thought. She braced herself for the inevitable pep talk.

'You know how much your father wants the team to do well today,' her mum said, selecting a pair of short dungarees from her wardrobe for Alice to wear. 'It's vital to his career as the school volleyball coach that the team gets to qualify for the final championships.'

'Yes, Mum,' she said.

'And it's just as important for you,' her mother added, hovering in the bathroom while Alice brushed her teeth. 'It'll be the start of your career as an athlete.'

Alice sighed inwardly. She couldn't deny that she enjoyed playing volleyball. On court, she had all the grace and confidence that seemed to elude her the rest of the time. She wasn't clumsy or fearful when she was playing a match – she was bold and decisive, with a natural sense of timing. Her parents took this as a sign that she was destined for sporting greatness, but Alice knew that volleyball wasn't her future. The only problem was that she hadn't told them yet.

'What's wrong?' her mother said. 'Aren't you happy to be following my footsteps? In Daniel's?'

'Of course!' she said, forcing a smile.

Her mother meant well, but why did sport have to be the only thing her family cared about? Not a day went past when she wasn't reminded that she was the daughter of an Olympic champion, or that her brother was a hero on the football pitch. It didn't help that she looked like a younger, slightly blonder version of her mother. Sometimes they all seemed to forget that she was an individual.

'The Keats family have a reputation to keep up,' her mum went on proudly. 'You wouldn't want to disappoint us, would you?'

'No,' she said softly.

'I haven't mentioned it to your dad,' her mother added in a confiding tone, 'but a few days ago I had a word with the head – and if the team qualifies today, she says you can be exempt from drama class to concentrate more on your training. Isn't that great news?'

'Yeah, great.' Alice smiled weakly. Inside she was crushed. *Forget about* Romeo and Juliet. *Forget about Thomas.*

Her mother looked at her quizzically. 'Good luck,

honey. I've washed and ironed your kit. You'll look the business when you go out on court.'

Alice unchained her bicycle like a sleepwalker and cycled to school like she was heading off a cliff. Too bad that she had forgotten to close her gym bag properly, too bad that her clean T-shirt slipped out and got caught in the wheels on the way. Too bad she now had to go on court with an oily tyre streak across her back. Another day, yet another #embarrassingmoment for Disaster Keats.

Andrea stood at the bus stop next to Jay, saying Thomas's name over and over again.

'Will you stop it?' Jay said. The repetition was driving him crazy.

'But it doesn't make sense.'

'What doesn't?'

'Any of it.'

She explained how she, Amber and Alice had created a perfect boy called Thomas Anderson on Real Life. 'We chose a drawing off the Internet for his profile photo. Then he turned up at school looking exactly like the drawing. How is that possible?'

Jay thought about it. 'Maybe it's a coincidence.'

'But how? The profile came to life too! We created our dream boy and now he's a living, talking person.'

It didn't make sense to Jay either, but he knew

there had to be a sensible explanation. 'Maybe Thomas did the drawing himself and you found it online by accident,' he suggested. 'Have you asked him? Shall I ask him for you?'

'No!' Andrea snapped. 'I mean, don't worry, I'll ask him.'

Jay was quiet for the rest of the journey, and Andrea felt bad. It wasn't his fault that she hadn't told him the whole story. He couldn't possibly guess that she had drawn the portrait of Thomas, ruling out his theory that it could all be a coincidence. Jay knew almost everything about Andrea, but he had no idea that she had loved drawing and painting as a child, or that she still secretly sketched. No one knew. She had given up art for science years ago. And that wasn't going to change.

Edward Bradford-Taylor was waiting on his motorbike outside Amber's house as she left for school. Her heart lurched when she saw him. For a moment she was lost in his gorgeousness – his dark blonde hair, the slant of his eyes. Then she remembered how easily his lips curled into a sneer . . . and she couldn't forgive him for saying that she kissed like a snail, either.

'Want a ride?' he asked.

It was tempting, but. . .

'Not from you,' she said.

He was stung. Like Amber, Edward Bradford-Taylor was used to getting what he wanted. 'Just from someone you don't know, huh?'

She smirked. He must have heard about her getting a ride home from Thomas. 'Jealous?'

He scowled. 'Why would I be? By the way, you'd better sign up on the board if you want to audition for the part of Juliet.'

She was surprised. 'Which board? There's nothing on Real Life. I looked.'

Now Edward was smiling. 'The drama class noticeboard, of course, where three people have already signed up before you – and one of them is May Rodriguez.' He put on his helmet, ready to go.

Amber didn't react to the mention of May Rodriguez, who she knew was a brilliant actress. She was too busy thinking about how to irritate Edward.

'Don't think I'll get back with you in exchange for the part of Juliet,' she warned.

'Who said I wanted to get back with you?' he said, revving his bike up.

He roared off, leaving Amber to search for a taxi.

The whole school seemed to know about Alice's stained sports shirt. She faced the usual humiliating stares as she trudged towards her locker, trying to rise above this latest embarrassment. In the hallway, Lynn and Jess darted scornful looks at her.

'Hi Alice, you *stain* long?' Lynn said with a snigger.

Opening her locker with a heavy heart, she was surprised to see a copy of the *Romeo and Juliet* script among her things. She whirled around wondering if Lynn and Jess had put it there, but they were gone. Then she noticed a note stuck to the script cover. On it was written, 'For my Juliet. May your dreams come true.' They were the exact words that Thomas had spoken in her dream. How could it be possible? Lynn and Jess had nothing to do with it. Which meant... Had Thomas left the script in her locker?

Hugging the script close, she ran off to find a secret place to read it. As she passed the maths classroom, she heard her name being called out on the register, but she didn't care. Soon she was alone in a storage room, going through the text, trying out Juliet's lines. She was amazed how easily they came to her – and stayed with her. It was almost as if they had been written for her.

Amber made sure that everyone saw her signing up for the Juliet audition. She wrote her name with a flourish at the bottom of the list, took a photo of the board and told Lynn and Jess to post it on Real Life.

JESS BAGLEY

To all the other wannabe Juliets: it's never too late to pull out.

43

You wouldn't want to embarrass yourself in front
of the class!

The message was clear: Back off and leave the part
to Amber!

A group of admirers gathered around their queen
bee. 'Will Edward be your Romeo?' they asked eagerly.

Jess stepped in. 'Girls, you should know that
Edward and Amber—'

'We're not together any more,' Amber said. 'So I'm
hardly going to kiss him in front of the whole school.'

As she walked away, flanked by her sidekicks, the
others huddled around to talk about her. 'I heard she's
going out with Thomas Anderson, the new student,'
someone said.

'Have you seen him? He's totally hot.'

'So he'll be her Romeo?'

'Amber Lee Thompson has all the luck!'

'Calling Alice Keats!'

Alice bolted out of the storeroom like a frightened
fawn when she heard her name being called on the
school loudspeaker system. *What if the head gives me
another punishment? I shouldn't have skipped a lesson to
read the play script!* she thought.

She raced to the head teacher's office, just in time

to see Andrea coming through the door, hanging her head. 'Don't say anything about Thomas,' Andrea whispered as they passed one another.

Alice went in, quaking with fright. 'Alice Keats,' said Mrs Barnes, and nodded at a man in police uniform.

'Miss Keats, I would like to have a word with you about last Friday,' the policeman said gravely. 'You were in detention in the library a few hours before the fire started, I believe. With Andrea Tanaka and Amber Lee Thompson?'

'Yes,' Alice said nervously.

'Don't worry, I just want to know if you noticed anything unusual,' he reassured her.

Alice answered his questions and left without mentioning Thomas or the profile they had created for him. She wondered what Andrea had said.

Andrea was in one of the study rooms plotting how to get back to the head teacher's office without being seen. Normally, she would have been fascinated by the police investigation into the fire, which they clearly suspected was a case of arson. But while she dutifully answered his questions, she had been distracted by an open file on the head teacher's desk – and the moment she realized that it was Thomas Anderson's file, she lost all interest in the police.

I have to see it! She was certain that it would reveal the hidden key to Thomas's origins.

She didn't notice Dylan Simmons slouched over a desk in the corner of the room, trying his best to disappear. The study room was the last place anyone would expect to find the school's worst student – and Dylan wanted to put off the police questioning for as long as possible. So here he was, hiding out, silently going over his alibi.

'I skipped out of detention early to go to band practice,' he would say. 'If you don't believe me, ask my girlfriend, Megan, or the other girls who were in the library. One of them even tried to stop me leaving. So I was nowhere near the library when the fire started.'

What he wouldn't say was that he had gone back after everyone else had left to pick up the band playlist he had forgotten. Or that he had found a letter from the head teacher requesting an urgent meeting with his parents. And he definitely would not reveal that he had used a lighter to set fire to the letter, thrown it in the waste paper basket while it was still burning, and left the library without looking back.

'Have you any idea what could have caused the fire?'

'Not a clue,' he would say.

Alice bumped into Amber on her way out of the head teacher's office. 'I didn't say anything about Thomas,' she whispered.

Amber barely glanced at her. 'I don't even know who you are,' she said, her green eyes narrowing as she pushed past. 'Don't ever speak to me again.'

As if I have time for a stupid police inquiry, she huffed, as the policeman went through his list of questions.

While Amber sulked, Alice walked back to her locker to return the play script. As she was closing the door, a hand grabbed hers.

'I've been looking for you,' Thomas said, leading her along the hallway. 'Come on.'

She would have gone anywhere with him, absolutely anywhere. Except that she was wearing the pair of dungarees that her granny had given her for her last birthday! Worse, along with the two spots on her nose, her long blonde hair was scraped back into an unflattering ponytail.

I'm a mess, she thought wretchedly. Self-esteem self-destruct!

As they entered a courtyard on the other side of the school, she looked up at the sky and begged the universe to strike her down with lightning.

Thomas clasped her hand tightly. 'If I profane with my unworthiest hand this holy shrine, the gentle sin is this. . .' he said.

She recognized the words from one of Romeo's speeches. She panicked. *This scene ends with a kiss! What do I do?*

'My two lips, two blushing pilgrims, ready stand to smooth that rough touch with a tender kiss. . .' He raised her hand to his lips.

Suddenly she knew what to do. 'Good pilgrim,' she said, the words flowing naturally, 'you do wrong your hand too much, which mannerly devotion shows in this, for saints have hands that pilgrims' hands do touch, and palm to palm is holy palmers' kiss.'

As their palms touched, a shiver went through her. 'You read the script,' Thomas said, sounding pleased.

'Yes!' she said excitedly, clothes, spots and self-esteem all forgotten. 'I shut myself in a storage room when I should have been in my maths class and I read it from top to bottom and back again, three times over, and I learnt it all by heart because I'm really good at memorizing things and always have been, even when I was a little girl. . .' She stopped to draw in a breath, her heart pounding, and realized in the silence that followed that she'd been jabbering. 'Sorry.'

He looked at her so intently that she could hardly bring herself to return his gaze. 'Alice,' he said softly, 'I want to act with you in the play. Shall we sign up for the auditions together?'

The simple beauty of the moment made her melt. But then her mother's words from earlier shot through her like bullets. She thought about the volleyball championships, her father's career and how proud her parents were. There was no way she could let them down.

'Sorry, I can't,' she said, her heart breaking. She turned and ran as hard as she could, away from Thomas and back into somebody else's dreams.

Later that day, Alice scanned the faces in the crowd as she walked out onto the volleyball pitch, looking for Thomas. He hadn't come. Was it because she had run away? 'Just stay calm,' her dad was telling everyone. 'In the end, it's only a game.'

Alice wasn't nervous about the match. She figured that if they won, her parents would be happy. If they lost, she could try out for *Romeo and Juliet* with Thomas.

'Of course, if we lose,' her dad added at the last minute, 'we'll be out of the championships and bring shame upon the whole school.'

'Thanks, that really helps,' Jess said sarcastically.

The match began and Alice played automatically, relying on the instincts she had honed over years of enforced practice. It struck her that she could get what she wanted if she deliberately messed up the game. A net foul, a double hit – it wouldn't take much more than that to swing the result. Then, what? No final championships, no non-stop training. She and Thomas could try out for the play and act together. . .

'Wake up, Keats!' one of her teammates yelled, just in time to alert her to a ball coming her way. She jumped up and spiked it as hard as she could over the net, winning the point.

No. She couldn't mess up. It wouldn't be fair on the team or her parents. She had to play to win. As she smashed another ball on target, the crowd cheered. 'Yes!' she yelled, high-fiving her teammates.

Andrea skipped the match. Instead, she waited in a hallway, just around the corner from the head teacher's office, until she heard the door click and saw Mrs Barnes step out with Rachel, the librarian. She watched until they were out of sight, then slipped into the office. She scanned the room for Thomas's file, her skin prickling with nerves. It was still on the desk where she had seen it. She picked it up and was just about to open it when she heard a voice. 'What are you doing?'

She dropped the file onto the desk with a gasp, upsetting a mug. Coffee spilled onto the desk and trickled over the cover of Thomas's file. She turned, expecting to see Mrs Barnes's frowning face, but it was Thomas standing in the doorway. 'Get out of here, Andrea,' he urged her softly. 'Mrs Barnes is on her way back. If she finds you here you can say goodbye to your Yale summer classes.'

She didn't need telling twice. 'Thanks,' she said, dashing towards the door.

Then she hesitated. How did Thomas know that

she was planning to take summer classes at Yale? She spun around to confront him.

But Thomas had vanished.

Alice stared at the empty court. The game was over. Her team was through to the semi-finals. She could hear her father on the phone to her mother, telling her how well their daughter had played. Alice knew she was lucky to have such a great family, yet it was hard to share their excitement. She was glad to have made him happy. She wanted to hug him. They had always been close. But she didn't know how to tell him she didn't want to be on the team any more. *Telling Mum will be even harder*, she thought miserably.

'She's inherited your killer timing,' he was saying. 'We couldn't have won it without her. I can't wait to see her back on court in the semis.'

Her dad came over and gave her a huge hug. 'Your mum's so proud of you! As of tomorrow, it's nothing but training for you,' he said fondly.

He obviously thought it would add to Alice's happiness, but it only left her feeling even more disconnected. 'Alice? Are you listening, kiddo?'

'Since the day I was born, Dad,' she replied, thinking about all the times in her past that her choices had been made for her by other people.

The changing rooms felt like a prison when she went

in. Her team had won, but she had lost her freedom. 'Why do none of them seem to notice that I'm not jumping for joy too?' screamed a voice in her head.

Suddenly a real scream echoed through the air. May Rodriguez was standing in front of her locker mirror with a look of horror on her face. Her cropped brown hair was now a radioactive shade of blonde. 'First I miss three smashes, now this. What's happening?' May wailed, bursting into tears. She buried her head in her hands. The rest of her teammates looked at one another in dismay. All except two.

'May?' Sonja said, going to comfort her.

'Go away,' May sobbed. Just then, she caught sight of Lynn and Jess, grinning nastily. 'Ugh, it was you two, wasn't it?' she said tearfully.

'Amber will do anything to win, including getting you two to ruin my hair because I wouldn't back off like all the other Juliets!'

Jess shrugged. 'It's not our fault you don't know the difference between shampoo and toilet cleaner.'

'Smile, you're on Real Life,' said Lynn, holding up her phone. She took a photo of May with tears pouring down her cheeks.

Maybe I'm better off out of the play, Alice thought. *Nobody wins when they go up against Amber.*

Heart against mind

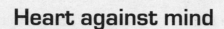

The photo of May soon went viral. Outside school, Amber was reading through Lynn's sneering comments when she heard a voice behind her.

'So I was right. You'd do anything to get the part,' Edward said.

She whirled round. 'You think I had something to do with it?'

'Does it matter?' he said. 'Amber Lee Thompson always gets what she wants. That's what I like about you.'

'Really? Well, get this, I don't like *anything* about you.'

'You like Anderson now, right?' he said. 'But Anderson doesn't know you like I do, Amber.'

'If you really knew me, you'd know that's not the way I operate!' she spat.

'What's bothering you? Lynn and Jess did something without asking your permission, is that it?'

She turned away. As she walked towards the school gates, it occurred to her that her classmates would assume she had put Lynn and Jess up to it. People saw her as ruthless. In their eyes, she was popular, but cruel. Was she really that person? And was it her fault that they wanted her to be their queen, despite it all?

Alice made her way towards the drama class. She had made up her mind to give up drama and concentrate on her volleyball training. She was determined not to regret it. A message flashed up on her phone.

THOMAS ANDERSON
Meet me outside the drama class? We'll sign up to audition together. ♥

She gasped. He had signed off with an emoji-heart!

Andrea sat in her bedroom, poring over a flow chart, her brown eyes squinting with confusion. She had meticulously set out a breakdown of the timings, accurate to the second. But whichever way she looked at it, she just could not make sense of Thomas's disappearance from the office. The inescapable fact was that there was a single exit. No back door. No window. No hole in the ceiling. Yet Thomas had somehow managed to vanish into thin air. *It's not possible*, Andrea insisted to herself. *What am I missing?*

'Houdini,' she typed into her search engine, 'the history of disappearing.'

*

In the drama-class dressing rooms, Jess and Lynn were pressuring May to skip the audition. 'Just leave me alone!' she told them.

'Ooooh,' they chorused, nastily.

The door burst open and in barged Amber, her hair completely hidden by a stylish tweed cap. 'Out, you two!' she told Lynn and Jess. Her sidekicks made a quick exit.

May stared at her coldly, then Amber took off her cap to reveal a cloud of completely white hair.

'You bleached your hair?' May said, gaping at her. 'Why?'

'What happened wasn't fair. I wanted us to compete on an equal footing.'

'Th-thank you,' May stammered.

'I still intend to get the part,' Amber said. 'But I'll get it because of my acting skills, not my hair colour.'

May made a great Juliet, but everyone watching the audition agreed that Amber had killed it. Midway through her audition, Edward posted his decision on Real Life.

EDWARD BRADFORD-TAYLOR
Who cares about the hair? I just found my Juliet.

Afterwards, he went backstage just as Amber took off her white wig.

'I knew it,' he said with a grin. 'It was a wig. This is the real Amber – and I like her.'

Flushed with the excitement of performing, she turned to him, eyes blazing. 'What do you want?'

'You,' he said coolly. 'Come on. . . I'll give you a ride home.'

Amber felt a rush of confusion. However much she thought she hated him, something always drew her back. Wondering why she was agreeing, she said, 'Fine.'

She had to dodge his arm around her shoulders as they approached the student parking bay. Then Edward saw his motorbike. 'My new tyres are flat!'

Suddenly Thomas appeared. 'Problems?' he asked wryly.

'You!' Edward rushed at Thomas, grabbed the collar of his jacket and raised his fist. 'You did this! Why? So you could take her home?'

'Hey, break it up!' Amber shouted, trying to get between them.

'Did you tell her what you did to May?' Thomas asked.

Edward froze. 'How do you know?'

Amber stared at him. Everything clicked into place. Edward was behind Lynn and Jess's trick on May. He'd given Lynn the bleach. He hadn't really wanted May to audition, despite his taunts that morning outside Amber's house. She and her rival had never been on an equal footing. Ugh.

'You sicken me, Edward,' she said, walking off.

When Thomas caught up with her, she was crying. 'Hey,' he said gently.

'Do you have any idea how I feel?' she asked him.

His dark eyes shone. 'I know exactly how you feel. And, for what it's worth, you would have got the part anyway, because you deserved it.'

'But Edward...'

'Edward doesn't know the real Amber. He can't even begin to see the beauty inside you.'

Amber's cheeks flushed and she shut her eyes. 'Do you really mean that?' she asked at last, looking at him through her long lashes.

But Thomas had gone.

Alice's acting dreams evaporated further when she read about Amber's audition success on Real Life. She hurried on to the drama office, determined to quit the class before she changed her mind.

Choose love! urged her heart.

Duty calls, said her head.

'Then plainly know my heart's dear love is set on the fair daughter of rich Capulet,' a voice said softly. 'As mine on hers, so hers is set on mine.'

She turned quickly. 'Thomas?' He was standing in

the hallway smiling at her, his hands in his pockets, his dark hair falling over his face.

'I waited for you, but you didn't come, so I signed us up to audition for extras anyway,' he said with a hint of mischief in his eyes.

'But I can't audition!' she protested. 'Drama class clashes with volleyball practice.'

He shrugged. 'You'll find a way to do them both.'

To her horror, he leaned forward, and whispered in her ear. 'You owe it to yourself to be the real Alice, to be true to yourself and your destiny. It's time to follow your true path – if acting is what you want to do, then do it.'

She stared at him, utterly bemused.

'I'll be with you,' he said, holding her face in his hands.

A sense of calm washed over her as she closed her eyes and waited for his lips to touch hers. *Kiss me*, she thought. *I'm not scared any more.*

There was a pause. Where was the kiss? She opened her eyes. Thomas had disappeared.

'Hey, loser.' Amber had rounded the corner and was striding towards her.

'Thomas?' Alice felt dizzy. She stared blankly at Amber. 'What are you talking about?'

'He was here – but he just vanished.'

'People don't vanish,' Amber said dismissively, even though he had done it to her. Alice watched in dismay as

Amber grabbed a pen, crossed out his name on the 'Extras' audition list and put him down for Romeo. 'Forget about Thomas Anderson,' Amber said, flicking her hair. 'You're way too drippy for him – and anyway, he's mine.'

Out of nowhere, Alice felt a surge of anger rising up inside her. 'He's not yours!' she cried.

'What did you say?' Amber snapped.

'Er, nothing,' she mumbled, her sudden courage deflating.

'I thought not. Bye, loser.' Amber turned her back and strutted off.

That word again. Loser. Alice's anger surged back. 'We created his profile together!' she yelled after her. 'Thomas is my ideal boy, too. He doesn't only belong to you.'

Amber spun round to face her. 'What?'

As she was about to launch herself at Alice, her phone beeped. So did Alice's. They both had the same message on their screen.

ANDREA TANAKA
We need to meet and talk about Thomas. This is all too crazy. I need your help. Tomorrow, before school? 8 a.m.?

Meanwhile in the library, Rachel was using a new computer when a picture of Thomas flashed up on the screen. She recognized him immediately. 'Oh no, not you!' she said, backing away in alarm.

'Something else about Thomas is puzzling me,' Andrea said, turning to her computer. 'I've done some research online and found out that the address in his file is an empty warehouse. Don't you think that's strange? Why would he lie about where he lives?'

Jay sighed. He'd come over to Andrea's house to take her to school, not to hear about Thomas again. 'Don't you think you're getting a little obsessed?'

'Negative,' she said, knowing in her heart that he was right.

The thing was she had every reason to obsess over Thomas Anderson – and it was nothing to do with his good looks or brilliant brain. His origins were clouded in mystery and he had vanished before her eyes – surely that was reason enough to spend sleepless nights and most of her waking hours trying to work out who he really was?

'So you don't like him, then?'

'Me? Him? Nah.'

Then she asked Jay if he would help her search for Thomas's empty warehouse during their lunch break.

'You don't have to. I mean, it could – I don't know, maybe it's dangerous,' she said.

He chuckled. 'When have I ever said no to you?'

*

She was late to meet Amber and Alice in the changing rooms. Amber was furious. Only *she* was allowed to be late. 'So what did you want to tell us about Thomas?' she asked impatiently.

Andrea's eyes grew wide. 'Thomas vanished in front of me,' she said.

The others looked at her, astonished.

'I can see in your faces that you know exactly what I'm talking about,' she continued. 'So what's going on? Either we're all having the same hallucination, or something else is happening here.'

There was a long pause. It just sounded so ridiculous.

Amber folded her arms across her chest. 'We're listening.'

'Have either of you even asked yourselves who Thomas is? Where he comes from?' Andrea asked them. 'I've searched online, but all I found was a video of a play he did at his last school. There's nothing else.' She didn't mention his fake address and the empty warehouse.

'So I was thinking we should start following him to see if he does anything strange.'

'I'm in!' agreed Alice.

'OK, but on one condition,' Amber said. 'If we don't find anything out, you'll back off and leave him to me.'

'Of course. He doesn't interest me – in that way,' Andrea said.

'Is that really true, Andrea?' Alice said. 'I mean, you were the one who started writing his profile. You found his picture. He's your ideal boy as well.'

'There are too many unanswered questions,' Andrea said. 'Anyway, I don't want a boyfriend.'

Alice took a deep breath. 'Well, I really like Thomas and I'm not giving him up for anyone,' she said, steeling herself for a fight with Amber.

'You?' Amber laughed softly. 'I'm not worried about you. See ya!'

Alice crumpled. As Amber strolled towards the door, her cashmere top falling prettily off her shoulders, her stunning red hair framing her perfect face, Alice knew she could never be a rival to the school queen bee.

Amber started hatching a plan as she headed off down the hallway. *I don't care whether he's a boy, a ghost or an alien*, she thought, *I want Thomas to be my Romeo in the school play*.

Her phone beeped.

EDWARD BRADFORD-TAYLOR
I need to see you. Can you meet me this morning? It's important.

AMBER LEE THOMPSON
No!

Fine, but I expect to see you at the auditions. So
make sure you come.

Edward had just finished fencing practice in the gym
of his Knightsbridge home. 'Let's go,' said James, his
training partner. 'We're going to be late for class.'

Edward put down his phone. 'Practice isn't over,
James. Get in position.'

'But—'

Edward put on his fencing mask and raised his foil.
He was spoiling for a fight – but if he wanted to be
truly powerful, he needed to channel his aggression.
That's why fencing was the best kind of discipline for a
guy like him, especially as today he planned to get his
revenge on Thomas. . .

. . .and win back Amber, the only girl he had ever
loved.

Since she didn't have a class until ten, Alice was first
on detective duty. But although she had seen dozens
of crime drama programmes with Grandma Keats,
trailing Thomas turned out to be a lot harder than
she'd imagined. She didn't have a clue how to make
herself invisible.

Amber was not remotely surprised to hear later that
Alice had tripped over a cleaner's bucket, fallen down

a flight of stairs and landed on a pile of gym mats with her legs in the air. What did amaze her was that she had managed to escape being photographed by James, who had witnessed the whole thing with Daniel.

'Your sister is really something,' James said to Daniel, shaking his head.

'This is going on Real Life.' He fumbled for his phone, but Alice was determined not to star in another #embarrassingmoment. Scrambling to her feet, she fled before he had time to take a picture. She pushed open the double doors of an emergency exit. They slammed behind her and the safety lock clicked, trapping her outside.

She messaged Daniel, but he refused to go to her rescue.

ALICE KEATS
Please? I could get suspended.

DANIEL KEATS
You're hopeless. I'll come during my lunch break.

She slid to the floor. Where was Thomas when she needed him?

AMBER LEE THOMPSON
Leave it to me, blockhead.

Now it was Amber's turn to follow Thomas.

She was hiding behind a row of lockers when she saw him coming out of class. Just then, somebody called her name. Bill Martin stood next to her, way too close for comfort. 'I heard you and Edward aren't together any more,' he said with a smile. 'I'm taken at the moment, but I could easily make myself free for you.'

'Too bad, Bill, I'm also taken,' she said.

Thomas was moving into another hallway now and Amber darted after him. Someone grabbed her arm. 'Hey!'

'Not now, Jess,' she said, shaking her off.

'But have you seen this?'

One glance at the picture on Jess's phone was enough to stop her in her tracks. It was a poster advertising the auditions for Romeo – the image of Juliet had Amber's face superimposed and the image of Romeo had Edward's.

'How dare he?' she spluttered. 'I'll bet he's planning to give himself the part of Romeo. Jerk!'

She messaged Andrea.

AMBER LEE THOMPSON
Your turn, Tanaka. I've got things to do.

In the school auditorium, Edward was flexing his director's muscles. He had already dismissed several potential Romeos by the time Amber arrived. Standing on the stage with a sword in his hand, he called, 'Next!'

When Bill Martin stepped up onto the stage, he laughed in disbelief. 'Is this a joke? It's Shakespeare, not a pie-eating contest.'

Amber ran to the stage. 'Edward, what are you up to?' she demanded. 'Why is your face on the poster?'

'At last Juliet graces us with her presence!' he sneered. 'Relax, it doesn't mean anything.'

Well, that's obviously a lie, she thought, as she watched him test Bill on his fencing skills, knocking his prop sword out of his hand within seconds. There were only about fifteen people watching the auditions, but Edward took a sweeping bow anyway, and was rewarded with loud applause.

'As I said before, the duel between Romeo and Tybalt is a crucial scene,' he declared. 'So anyone who doesn't know how to handle a sword should forget about the role.'

Double jerk! Amber thought. So this was how he intended to eliminate his rivals. Edward was the school fencing champion – no one could compete with his sword skills. If he had his way, she was going to have to say some of the most romantic lines ever written to a boy she was beginning to outright hate.

*

Andrea proved to be an excellent detective, ducking, diving and hiding behind bushes in the school gardens. However, Thomas turned out to be an incredibly boring suspect. During the hour she was following him, he did nothing to arouse suspicion. He drank water, ate a snack, got a book out of his locker, sat on a bench and read it . . . yawn.

She thought she had lost him at one point, but then she spied him talking to Rachel, the librarian. Now that was strange. How did he know Rachel? She moved in closer to eavesdrop. 'Yes, it's on a library computer,' he was saying.

Hey, why was he talking about the school computer? That was where everything began, where Thomas had been invented. Did he know that?

Like it or not, Andrea realized, she, Amber and Alice were all in this together. They had created the profile of Thomas together – and they had to solve the mystery together. So there could be no more holding back information from them. They needed to check out his fake address in Chinatown, while Jay stayed at school to keep an eye on Thomas for them.

The trouble with love...

The first dead end came during the search for Thomas's address in Chinatown. Andrea's map led them to a windowless warehouse that definitely did not look inhabited. They knocked on nearby doors to ask if anyone knew Thomas, but were met with blank stares.

'Let's try the warehouse, you never know,' Andrea said.

'This is going nowhere, Tanaka,' Amber complained.

Andrea banged on a red metal door. An old Chinese woman answered.

'We're student representatives of the London International High School and we're looking for Thomas Anderson's home address,' Andrea said.

'Come in, dears,' the old woman said, hustling them inside.

The door slammed behind them and they found themselves in a dark room with high ceilings.

'I don't know about this, girls!' Alice whimpered.

Behind her, she heard the old woman's voice say,

'We have a rule here. Nobody leaves without...' The girls spun round to see the woman holding up two dishes piled high with food and grinning broadly, '...tasting our fabulous food!'

Blinking to adjust their eyes to the darkness, they realized that they had accidentally stumbled into a Chinese restaurant.

'The students of the London International High School are very welcome here,' the old lady announced.

Dizzy with relief, they looked at each other and burst out laughing. There was nothing for it but to sit down and eat.

Back on the street, about a hundred courses of food later, Alice looked at her watch and freaked out. 'Volleyball practice, I have to go!' she said, sprinting off.

Amber turned to Andrea. 'I came on this wild goose chase because you said that if we didn't discover anything more about Thomas then you would leave him to me. Are we clear?'

Andrea frowned. 'You sound like my dad when he's on the phone doing a business deal!'

'Yeah, well, I guess my mother taught me how to negotiate,' Amber said. 'She has her own fashion company, so she knows how to strike a hard bargain.'

'And your dad?'

'He sets up eco-businesses,' she said brightly. 'I guess he's not so hardheaded. Hey, why am I telling you this? Just say you'll stay away from Thomas. And from me – OK?'

'Wait,' Andrea said.

'No,' Amber yelled. 'You may get the top grades in the school, but I'm the pro in love. It's obvious that you're in love with Thomas, but your chances of getting him are a big fat zero! Got that?' She stormed off to the audition.

Andrea wandered through Chinatown, questions buzzing through her head. Was Amber right? Did she think about Thomas all the time because she was really in love with him? It started raining. She put up her hood and walked on. A few moments later, she saw Thomas walking towards her through the drizzle, a large grey dog by his side. Wasn't he meant to be at school?

This is becoming so crazy I can't even begin to understand it, she thought.

'What do you say we get out of the rain?' Thomas said, as if it was the most normal thing in the world to bump into her like that.

Andrea shrugged. Why not? It was all so far-fetched that she might as well see where it took her.

As they walked along the street, she messaged Amber.

AMBER LEE THOMPSON

You'd better not be, for your own sake.

Three minutes later...

AMBER LEE THOMPSON

Actually, keep him there until the audition is
over. My plan will work better if he's not
here.

Thomas and his dog, Otto, took Andrea to a store
full of rare art and architecture books. To her delight,
it was a treasure trove of out-of-print titles and other
amazing volumes that she'd thought were impossible
to find. 'You don't know how incredible this is for me!'
she burst out. 'I didn't even know this shop existed.'

She started telling him about her dream to study
architecture, about her passion for structure and form.
I'm rambling, she thought.

She broke off. 'Can I ask you a question?'

'Sure.'

'Where do you live?'

He didn't even hesitate. 'Here, on the floor above
the bookstore, with my uncle,' he said. 'He owns

the building. When I was living in New York, I used to come here every summer. It's the only place that really feels like home to me, where I feel happy and free to be myself. My uncle owns a warehouse in Chinatown, too.'

'I see,' she said, surprised that he was being so open.

'Do you have a place where you feel happy and free?' he asked, stroking Otto.

Andrea's mind whirled back to her early childhood. A memory flashed into her mind, of the day she had first sat on the floor of her mother's art studio, paintbrush in hand, making splodges on a canvas. Where had that just come from?

She didn't try explaining it to Thomas. 'I don't need a special place where I can be myself, because I'm always myself, wherever I am,' she said defensively.

Thomas didn't seem to notice. He changed the subject. 'My uncle has asked me to re-catalogue a load of books,' he said. 'It's a ton of work. How about you help me? You'd get to look at all your favourite architecture books – and we could study together too.'

Andrea's mouth went dry. She cleared her throat. 'Er. . .' She had absolutely no idea of what to say or do. What would happen if she flung herself into his arms and hugged him tight? She shook her head, trying to clear her mind.

At last she found her voice. 'I have to go!' she croaked. 'I'm late for my photography class.'

'Wait, I'm coming too,' he said, following her as she hurried out of the shop.

On the bus back to school, she brooded over her inability to ask him all the questions that had been puzzling her. She felt more confused than ever. He was just so gorgeous and clever. His presence seemed to mess with her logical thought processes.

'May I?' he said, pointing at her camera. Their fingers brushed as she handed it over, sending an electric charge through her wrist and up her arm. He took a selfie of the two of them, sitting side by side, their mirror images reflected in the bus window.

At the Romeo audition, Edward was about to declare himself the only suitable candidate for the role.

'What about Thomas?' Amber asked.

'I don't see him anywhere, do you?' Edward asked, his eyes wide with fake innocence.

Amber gave a signal to Lynn and Jess and the stage curtains opened to reveal a cinema screen. 'Hey, what's this?' said Edward.

Soon everyone in the auditorium was transfixed by the video that Andrea had found online. Thomas was giving an extraordinary performance as Romeo, a part he had played in a school play in New York.

In no time, Real Life was humming.

HELEN MASON
Awesome! Awesome! Awesome!

SONJA CONSTANZA
He has to be Romeo!

There was no one who didn't want Thomas to play Romeo in Edward's production.

Amber caught Edward's eye when the screening ended. 'So what do you say, director?' she asked, hands on hips.

Edward was furious. Yet he had no choice but to go with popular opinion.

'I think we've found our Romeo,' he announced through clenched teeth.

Just then, Thomas walked into the auditorium. He was met with a huge round of applause. 'Did I miss something?' he asked, looking around in surprise.

'Haven't you heard?' Amber giggled. 'You're the luckiest guy in the school – you get to kiss me!'

Bill Martin thumped him on the back. 'Congratulations, you're Romeo, mate!'

In a shadowy corner of the auditorium, Alice burst

into tears. She hated the idea of Amber and Thomas kissing. *I should be his Juliet! Me!*

Andrea, too, felt her mood plunging when she read about the casting. No one doubted now that they were cast as Romeo and Juliet that Amber and Thomas were set to become the school golden couple. And yet... The way he had spoken to her earlier told a different story. Overcoming her shyness, she sent him a message on Real Life.

ANDREA TANAKA
You'll make a great Romeo. And if you
still have time, I'd like to help you
catalogue the books at the bookstore –
and study together. :)

For the first time in her whole life, she had ended a message with a smiley face. *What is happening to me?* she wondered. Lying in bed, half asleep, waiting to see if Thomas would reply, her heart thumped when she heard her phone beep.

JAY WILLIAMS
Are you still awake?

She was too disappointed to reply.
Down in the street below, Jay wistfully looked up

at her window. He could see her light was still on, so she was either ignoring him or so deep in her studies that she hadn't noticed the message on her phone. Except that had never happened before.

What am I doing here? he asked himself. *I'm an idiot. If I told her how I really felt about her, she'd probably never speak to me again.*

After loads of rehearsals, the big day was just one sleep away. Amber and Thomas were scheduled to practise the scene of Romeo and Juliet's first kiss. Everyone was talking about it on Real Life. Amber couldn't stop day-dreaming about it.

She had planned her day with characteristic precision. Every detail was covered, from the dress that would highlight the colour of her eyes to the flavour of her lip gloss. She was thinking peach, maybe cherry. In her mind she kept replaying kisses that hadn't actually happened yet.

Her friends were also in a state of excitement. Jess had agreed to create an amazing hairstyle for her. Lynn was on make-up duty. Best of all, Megan was writing a piece of music to accompany the moment – because everyone knew that there had to be a romantic song when the stars of a movie kissed for the first time, and how was this any different?

Amber barely slept, she was so psyched for the day to come. As she went to bed, she typed a final message.

AMBER LEE THOMPSON
Life is perfect #goodnight.

Alice and Andrea also had trouble sleeping, tossing and turning restlessly as they tortured themselves with visions of Amber and Thomas kissing.

Why can't it be me? Alice howled silently at the universe, crying bitter tears. She barely gave a thought to the crucial volleyball game she would be playing the next day – until she realized it clashed with the rehearsal. Why did she even want to go to the rehearsal? Just for more torture?

ALICE KEATS
Life is a disaster #goodnight.

It's a play, Andrea kept telling herself. *It's logical for them to kiss. It's part of the plot.* Instead of concentrating on her studies, she fiddled with her hair, doodled on her pad and stared into space. For the first time in her life, she didn't finish her homework before going to bed.

Life is confusing #goodnight.

*

Amber stamped her feet like a spoilt child. 'Mum, you don't understand how important this is to me!' Phase one of her plan was going badly.

'You're being dramatic, it's only a dress,' her mother said calmly.

'No, Mum, you're ruining my life!'

'Don't be silly. Let's put this in perspective, shall we? This is a thousand-pound dress and I won't let you borrow it – let alone go to school in it!'

'But I need something new!' Amber insisted. 'It's really important!'

'Darling, you have a wardrobe full of designer clothes. With a little imagination and clever styling, you could wear a new outfit every day for a year. I could show you how, if you like.'

'Forget it, you have no idea,' Amber yelled, stomping back to her bedroom.

I'll find something else to wear, she decided, *and when Thomas sees me he'll fall in love and then he'll kiss me and we'll be together and my perfect day will end perfectly!*

In the hallway outside the canteen, Alice saw Thomas getting something out of a locker. *It's a sign!* she thought. *I just have to tell him how I'm feeling. He can't kiss Amber at the rehearsals, he just can't!*

She walked towards him and then hesitated. *Go on!* She took another step forward and then retreated. *I can't!* She darted through the computer-room door.

'Calm down,' she said softly. As her breathing slowed, a passage from *Romeo and Juliet* came to her. *Wait*, she thought. *I could tell him outright, or I could use Juliet's lines.*

'In truth, fair Montague,' she said aloud, gaining confidence, 'I am too fond, and therefore thou mayst think my behaviour light. . . Therefore pardon me and not impute this, yielding to light love, which the dark night hath so discovered. . .'

It felt right. Now she needed to say it in her own words. She rushed out of the room with renewed courage.

From the back of the class, Edward had watched, unnoticed, as Alice's solo performance unfolded. *Alice Keats as Juliet?* Edward thought. *That's interesting.*

Amber's day was going from bad to worse. Now phase two of her plan wasn't working out. Little did she know, but Megan was trapped in the head teacher's office with her mother, Rachel. Megan was taking the rap for the library fire, knowing that Dylan would be expelled if the head found out it was really his fault. Her boyfriend had broken the rules so many times that he was already on borrowed time at London International High School.

'I know it was an accident, but I have no choice but to suspend you for two weeks,' Mrs Barnes said.

Megan hung her head. 'Of course.'

Mrs Barnes frowned. 'I'm sorry, Rachel,' she said to the librarian.

'Don't worry, you're doing what's necessary,' Rachel said. She turned to Megan. 'Do you understand how serious the consequences could have been?' she asked sharply.

Megan stayed silent.

Rachel knew the truth of what had happened, but her daughter had pleaded with her to support her version of events.

'I don't think you should have taken the blame for Dylan's carelessness,' Rachel said a few minutes later, as they got into her car outside the school. 'Are you sure he's the right boy for you? I don't want to interfere, my darling, but. . .'

'No, Mum,' Megan snapped. 'He's my boyfriend and he's going to stay my boyfriend. Just be cool with that, please.'

Outside the chemistry lab, Amber was desperately messaging Jess. Phase three of her plan had just imploded.

AMBER LEE THOMPSON

What about my hair? My make-up?

JESS BAGLEY

I waited for half an hour but you didn't
come!

AMBER LEE THOMPSON

Why didn't you come to my office? You
knew I was waiting for Megan there.

JESS BAGLEY

I did exactly what you told me to. Now I've got to
get ready for the game. I'm really, really sorry.

No dress, no romantic song, no hair and make-up.
What else could go wrong?

Her chemistry teacher appeared. 'You're late for
class, Lee Thompson!'

She put on her white coat and went to her bench.
On her right, May was mixing liquids in a test tube.
May's hair was looking awesome. She always styled it
really well. For a second, Amber contemplated asking
May for help. Not a good idea, she decided, after what
had happened with Lynn and Jess and the bleach. May
might get her revenge by turning her grey or something.

*

'I'd never use a wide angle, would you? That's for amateurs. No, it's 35 mm for me every time.'

Andrea yawned as Stuart, the school geek, ruined her lunch hour.

'Who do you think you are?' someone said threateningly.

Jay was standing in front of them, his hair swept back and his collar turned up, wearing sunglasses and sucking a lollipop. He looked like the coolest eighties throwback.

'Why are you sitting here with my girlfriend? Get up now!'

Andrea's eyes glinted with relief. Her silent cry for help had been answered. 'Ooh, babe, it's not what you think,' she said in her girliest voice.

'Get lost, shrimp,' Jay said. Stuart couldn't get away fast enough.

Jay and Andrea collapsed with laughter. 'You're a good friend, thank you,' she said. 'And you're very convincing in the jealous boyfriend role.'

Jay shrugged. 'No problem,' he said. 'You can count on me to protect you.'

Andrea giggled and kissed him on the cheek. 'You're my best friend in the world, you know.'

'Yeah,' he murmured as she wandered off. 'Your best friend, nothing more.'

'Aren't you coming?' she called.

'OK.' He went after her. 'Hey, what is it?' She was standing at the door, gazing dreamily at something – or someone – in the hallway. He followed her sight line and saw . . . Thomas Anderson. Always Thomas.

You? she wondered as she stared at Thomas. *What is your mystery? Who are you, really?*

'Andy?' Jay said, waving his hand in front of her vacant gaze. 'Are you there?'

She didn't answer. Instead, she raced after Thomas and was just in time to see him go into the drama classroom. Edward was there to greet him.

'Anderson, you're late,' he said curtly.

'Hi, Ed,' Thomas said.

'It's Edward to you!' he snapped. 'And what are you doing here, Tanaka?'

Andrea froze. 'Er, I was thinking of volunteering as set designer,' she said, improvising madly. 'I heard you decided to make it a minimalist production, is that right? Well, if you've seen any of my photography, you'll know I'm into minimalism in a big way – I mean, a small way . . . er, in a minimalist way?'

To her amazement, Edward fell for it. 'Hmm, OK, come in,' he said.

At the volleyball game, Alice was feeling torn again. She longed to be at the play rehearsal.

'Come onto the court, Alice!' her father called.

She stood up. 'You always seem to be in a dream these days,' he said, his voice full of concern. 'Is there anything wrong?'

'No, Dad,' she said glumly. *If only she could tell him. But what good would it do?*

'Focus,' he told her. 'Don't think about anything except winning.'

She tried, she really tried. But she couldn't escape the image of Thomas leaning towards her, his lips about to touch hers instead of Amber's. . . She shrieked in pain as a ball hit her hard in the face.

Her teammates rushed over to see if she was OK. 'Time out!' her father called. 'You need to see the nurse!'

'I'm fine, honestly, Dad.'

'Don't be silly. You're done for the day. Anyway, I don't want you on the court unless you're prepared to give a hundred per cent.'

'I'm sorry,' she said.

As soon as she was safely through the door and out of sight, she upped her pace and sprinted to the drama room.

In the chemistry lab, another round of bad news was coming through. Lynn messaged Amber to say that Edward was withholding the costumes.

AMBER LEE THOMPSON

You'd better find a way to bring one to me now!

LYNN JAVINS

I'll try! But I don't think you'll like it when you
see it.

AMBER LEE THOMPSON

What do you mean?

It was clear that Amber hadn't yet heard about
Edward's idea for a minimalist production, or that
he wanted the entire cast to be dressed in black-and-
white sacks. Lynn didn't relish the thought of breaking
the news to her.

Amber was too distracted to notice the chemistry
teacher looking over her shoulder. 'Miss Lee Thompson,
how is your experiment going?' he asked.

She mumbled an excuse and was infuriated when
the rest of the class sniggered. At that very moment,
her test tube erupted, splattering slime everywhere
and filling the air with yellow fumes.

'You've gone too far this time!' her teacher warned,
fanning away the pungent smell of sulphur. He
clapped his hands. 'The lesson is over for today,' he
announced. 'Off you go, everyone.' He gave Amber a
stern look. 'Except you, obviously.'

'But I have to get to my drama rehearsal!' she protested.

'Not until you've cleaned up this mess,' he said firmly, handing her a wet rag.

She had no choice but to obey. Her perfect day was turning into a nightmare.

The drama room was packed out. The rehearsal hadn't begun yet, and everyone was focused on Thomas as he talked about his old school and life in New York. There was a lot of boring stuff about his basketball training schedules, but Andrea listened intently. She longed to know more about him. Alice, too, was hanging on his every word, wondering when would be a good time to tell him how she felt. They were both dreading Amber's arrival, dreading the kiss! And yet neither could bring herself to walk away.

'OK, guys, time to start,' Edward said. 'As you all know, today we're going to be rehearsing the scene where Romeo and Juliet kiss.'

'That's going to be slightly difficult without our leading lady, Ed,' Thomas pointed out. He started drawing a face on the cardboard cup he was holding. 'Here, will she do?' he asked. 'Fair Juliet!' he cried, addressing the cup. Everyone laughed.

Edward scanned the room for Amber and

noticed Lynn edging towards the door with a costume. 'Where do you think you're going?' he demanded.

Lynn dropped the sack. 'Nowhere,' she stammered. 'I was just tidying up.'

'Tell me the truth!' he said.

Lynn gave up. 'Amber asked me to take it to her,' she admitted.

'Amber asked you? Where *is* Amber?'

For a perfectionist like Amber, this was a worst-case scenario. Her hands were stained yellow, the smell of sulphur clung to her hair and clothes and she was late. The life-changing moment that she had schemed so hard for was slipping out of reach. Unbelievably, her first kiss with Thomas might not actually happen.

So when Bill popped up stroking his goatee and calling her 'my queen!', Amber took the opportunity.

'I need you to clear this up for me while I go to drama rehearsal,' she said.

He surveyed the devastation. 'You think I'm an idiot?'

'I think you'd do it in exchange for being seen getting a milkshake together, in front of everyone. Am I wrong?'

She was never wrong. 'Tomorrow during break time?' he said hopefully.

In your dreams, Bill.

'Done,' she said.

Alice watched in horror as Thomas leaned in to kiss Lynn. *This is a nightmare.*

The door flew open and in burst Amber, screaming, 'Stop!'

Everybody turned to look at her. 'How dare you interrupt my rehearsal?' Edward snarled.

'What do you mean?' Amber shrieked. 'It's my scene! So what is Lynn doing onstage?'

Edward pointed at the clock on the wall. 'You were late! Actors have to be on time – or the curtain goes up with an understudy.'

Amber turned to Lynn, her eyes blazing with anger. 'Is this why you didn't come with my costume?'

'Of course not, I—'

'Cool it, both of you,' said Thomas, getting between them. 'Amber, go and get ready.'

Amber instantly calmed down. Of course her sidekick hadn't betrayed her – she wouldn't dare. 'All right. Lynn, come with me,' she said.

'Wait,' Edward said. 'I'm the director here! I make the decisions.'

But Amber was impatient to get ready. 'I'll go onstage when I get back, OK?'

'And if I say no?'

'You'll be sorry,' she threatened.

Edward smiled. Never a good sign. *What's he plotting now?* she wondered.

In the bathroom, Lynn helped her with her hair and make-up. 'I look a wreck!' Amber said, examining herself in the mirror. She wrinkled her nose and gave her sleeve a sniff. 'I stink, too. Where's my costume?'

Lynn started brushing her hair. 'Why don't you skip it? No one else is wearing theirs.'

'So I was right! You didn't try to bring it to me.' Amber scowled.

'I did!'

'Oh, forget it, I don't blame you for wanting to kiss Thomas.'

Lynn made a face. She wasn't interested in Thomas. 'It wasn't like that. I did it because Edward asked me to.'

'Edward! Ugh, what did I ever see in him?' She sprayed her hair with perfume.

'You two are fighting right now,' Lynn said, 'but he's not that bad, really – and he's a good director.'

Amber whirled around to face her. 'Whose side are you on?' she demanded.

Lynn drooped. 'Yours, obvs.'

'Give me my costume, then.'

Lynn reluctantly handed over one of Edward's sacks. Amber stared at it in disbelief. 'You are joking,' she said.

What happened next took the whole school by surprise . . .

PAM LARKIN
Amber's refusing to wear a sack! The queen
wants a dress.

BRUCE RIBEIRO
Thomas has gone.

LIZ LAPILLE
No kissing today, then?

BRITNEY STATON
Now Edward's telling Amber to rehearse the
scene with him.

JESS BAGLEY
She's refusing.

RODNEY LEE
Wow, it's a showdown between the king and

queen! He's saying he'll kick her off the show if
she doesn't rehearse with him.

JESS BAGLEY
AMBER HAS JUST WALKED OUT OF THE
PLAY!

LIZ LAPILLE
You should have seen how angry she was!

JESS BAGLEY
Will she come back? What now?

BRITNEY STATON
No way she'll be back.

BRITNEY STATON
But who will be Juliet? May? Lynn?

LIZ LAPILLE
YOU ARE NOT GOING TO BELIEVE THIS!
Edward has chosen his new Juliet.

BRUCE RIBEIRO
Ladies and gentlemen, I present to you ... the
one and only Alice Keats!

Do you or don't you?

Although it had been announced months earlier, everybody had forgotten about Stop Cyberbullying Day. So no one was prepared for Real Life going offline, which meant that there was a large number of headless chickens wandering around the London International High School campus.

Only Bill Martin was ready for the blackout. By eight thirty that morning, he had already set up a stall outside the main entrance selling paper and pens.

On her way to school, Andrea freaked when she noticed her phone wasn't connecting. 'What's wrong? This is a disaster. Come on!'

'Environmental pollution is a disaster,' Jay teased her as they walked through the school gates. 'In comparison, this is a blip on a blip on a micro-blip.' He looked at her. 'This sudden interest in Real Life wouldn't have anything to do with Thomas Anderson, would it?'

'What about Thomas?' she asked innocently.

'You tell me! All I know is that you're different since he came along.'

'Different, how?' she asked sharply.

'Just different! You signed up to be a set designer, even though you're not interested in the drama class – and you're going to his uncle's bookstore almost every day.'

'So?'

'You're in love with him, aren't you?'

'Of course I'm not!' she said. 'If you really need an explanation, I'm doing the scenery to get a good grade. You know my work comes before everything. And the bookstore has some of the books I need to write the essay for my Yale summer school application. You're a clever guy, Jay, but sometimes you can be so stupid!'

Jay's right, I am different, Andrea thought, as she reached into her locker.

Down the hallway, Alice was surrounded by a gaggle of admirers, cooing over her hair and clothes. 'Your dress is AMAZING! Where did you buy it?'

'I, er, it came from my cousin. It didn't fit her any more,' Alice said hesitantly.

'So it's vintage! How cool.'

'Are you ready for your epic kiss with Thomas

Anderson?' someone asked Alice. 'Girl, I'm soooo jealous!'

Is this what being popular feels like? Alice wondered.

Edward swept by with James in tow. 'Keats, rehearsals are about to begin!' he barked. 'Are you coming or not?'

'Yes!'

'And try not to have any accidents on the way,' he added scornfully.

Lynn stepped into his path and smiled. 'If you find yourself looking for a better Juliet, you know where to come,' she purred.

'Why, is Amber on her way?' he shot back.

She pouted angrily. 'Why do you care?'

'Forget it.' He disappeared around the corner.

Lynn turned to Jess, her expression full of spite. 'Did you see how full of herself Keats is getting?'

'Yeah, wait till Amber hears. She'll put a stop to it.'

'Wake up, Jess,' Lynn hissed at her. 'Haven't you heard what everyone's saying? Amber's reign is over. The queen has been deposed – and about time too.'

Amber was at home.

'I'm sick,' she told her mum.

'You don't look sick to me. Is something wrong?' her mother asked. 'I'm late for a meeting now, but can we talk about it later?'

'If you really want to,' Amber said, although she had no intention of telling her mother how she was feeling.

She picked up her phone and threw it down again. Without Real Life, it was useless. For the first day in months, she had no idea what people were saying about her and actually she couldn't care less, she decided. The play no longer concerned her. Her popularity was unimportant. The only thing that mattered was Thomas and what she was going to wear on their first proper date.

He had sent her a message the night before, saying he wanted to see her . . . that meant a date, right? He would show up at her door, flash a smile, whisk her away on his motorbike, take her for a moonlit picnic.

A flicker of doubt entered her head. What was he doing right now? Was he rehearsing with Keats? What if Alice's wide-eyed innocence won him over? She pictured them snuggled up on a park bench together, feeding the swans, walking along the river at sunset. . .

Fortunately for her sanity, Megan turned up, bubbling with enthusiasm as she told Amber about the new song she was writing. 'I wanted you to be the first to hear it!' she said, plugging in her iPod.

*

Alice and Thomas were onstage, wearing their sacks, rehearsing the balcony scene between Romeo and Juliet. They were surrounded by several columns of flimsy boxes that comprised Edward's minimalist set.

For the third time that day, as Alice leaned forward to say her lines, she lost her balance and collapsed into a pile of cardboard.

'Stop!' Edward yelled. 'Get it together, Keats. What was I thinking when I cast you?' he said. 'That's enough comedy for one day. Let's pick it up again tomorrow.'

Alice looked at Thomas in dismay. 'Hey, you didn't do so badly,' he reassured her. 'You just have to believe in yourself.'

He was so kind, so thoughtful, so totally perfect.

'See you tomorrow,' he added.

'Yeah,' she said shyly. She sighed happily as she watched him leave the room.

James strode up and handed her a piece of paper. 'Check this out, Keats.'

'What do you want, James?' she asked.

He shrugged and walked off. 'Just doing my job as assistant director. Thought you might want to see the rehearsal schedule.'

She looked down the list of dates and her heart sank. *Clash, clash, clash.*

Volleyball vs drama. 'But I can't do all these times!' she called after him.

'I'm fairly certain that's not my problem,' he replied.

How could I ever have liked you? she thought, heading for the exit. But James wasn't her problem, the schedule was. She was in mega-trouble. How could she keep her role in the play a secret now?

She pushed the door open and walked straight into her father. 'We need to talk,' he said solemnly.

Oh, great.

Against her better judgement, Andrea went to find Thomas on the football pitch, somewhere she wouldn't have been seen dead before he came along.

A group of superfans were standing behind the wire, cheering his every touch of the ball, shouting out how amazing and gorgeous he was.

'How do you manage to be so perfect?' one of them mused, just as Andrea passed by.

'Good question,' she said.

'Hey, what's the super-nerd doing here?' someone said.

Just then, Thomas tackled Daniel, won the ball and scored a goal. 'Your sister's boyfriend is really something, Daniel!' someone said.

Daniel was quick to correct him. 'He's not her boyfriend. They're just acting together.'

Andrea made her move while Thomas was taking

time out for a drink of water. 'Hey,' he said, smiling as he looked up and saw her.

She swallowed awkwardly. 'So I was wondering, you see – er, I'm here because I couldn't message you on Real Life – so, then, I need a book for my essay, and I was thinking maybe the bookstore had it, and so if I go there tomorrow...' *Help, I'm rambling*, she thought.

'...you could get the book and we could study together,' he said, finishing the sentence for her. 'Great idea.'

Andrea's heartstrings zinged. Was it that easy?

'I guess I should go back on the pitch,' he said. 'See you tomorrow?'

'Thanks,' she said, trying, but failing, to say more. Why couldn't she just add, 'It was good to see you'? What was wrong with her?

She saw Jay walking across the grass towards her. 'Bad move, shape-shifting alien,' he said with a chuckle. 'The real Andrea would never have gone to a football match, not even if Einstein was playing. So the question is, what have you done with her?'

'Cut it out!' she said.

He gave her a sad look and held out a drink carton. 'Come on, I even brought you a milkshake. I wanted to get you lunch, but three o'clock is a bit late—'

'Three?' she repeated. 'I'm late for my mother's art preview! I said I'd help her organize it. She'll kill me!'

'See you later?' he called as she ran off.

'I'll write when Real Life is online again,' she called back.

What do I do now? What on earth do I do?

As she cycled home from school, Alice went over her conversation with her father. 'But why didn't you tell us?' he had asked. 'After all, it's not a walk-on part – you're playing the lead!'

'It's just not that important,' she'd replied, looking at the ground. 'I only go to one rehearsal a week.'

'Don't forget that we have a championship to win,' he said. 'If we're going to make it, you have to focus.'

'I know, Dad. Nothing will distract me from it,' she'd assured him. 'I promise.'

Was that true, though? She replayed the rehearsal in her head. She definitely wasn't anywhere near good enough to play Juliet. Edward had chosen her on a whim, to spite Amber, and now he was regretting it – because she was the most ridiculous candidate for Juliet of all time.

Thomas had reassured her, but was he being sincere? He was probably only saying it because he liked her. *If* he liked her. She knew she needed to ask him outright, but when would she get the chance?

Her stomach began to make rumbling noises. She hadn't eaten anything since lunchtime – it was definitely time to go home. Looking around to get her bearings, she realized that she had stopped right outside the Brick Lane Theatre. She had seen several shows there with her old school, years before. She remembered it as a place of magic and sparkle, where fantastical stories came to life on the stage – and it struck her as a weird coincidence, because it had been right there that she had first started dreaming about being an actor.

She hadn't cycled past it for ages, and now it looked like it had been boarded up. *It must have closed down*, she thought sadly. She parked her bike against a wall so that she could take a closer look. There was a gap under the wooden boards blocking one of the exits. She crouched down and crawled through it. Stepping into the airy auditorium was like entering another world.

'Wow,' she said aloud. It was a breathtakingly beautiful space, with wood-panelled walls, Greek-style columns, an ornate gilded stage and rows of red velvet seats. It was every bit as magical as she remembered.

Andrea arrived at her mother's gallery intending to stay just long enough to help out, admire the art and say hello to a couple of her parents' friends.

'Darling!' her mother said, putting a firm arm around her and pushing her towards a boy with purple highlights in his curly hair. 'This is Ralph.'

Andrea smiled weakly at Ralph, trying hard not to show her irritation. So it was just another one of her mother's traps! How predictable — she should have guessed.

'Well, hello,' Ralph gurgled, his voice a complete contrast to his hipster clothes and cool specs. He held up an embossed box and said, 'Would you like to see my insect collection?'

What a weirdo! How do I get away? she thought. *I wish you were here to rescue me, Thomas.*

'Yes, I always carry it with me,' Ralph babbled on. 'People find it so fascinating.'

'Do they, really?'

She heard a voice say, 'Hi Andrea.'

No, it couldn't be.

A hand grazed her knuckles. She turned around. *Yes, it was.* Thomas was standing behind her.

She gulped. 'How did you know I was here?'

Megan sat on the bed in Amber's bedroom trying to help her friend choose the perfect outfit for her date with Thomas.

'Nope,' Megan said to an orange playsuit that matched Amber's hair. 'You look like a goldfish.'

Next Amber put on a navy calf-length dress that miraculously transformed her into ... 'a human penguin?'

Amber changed again – into a cream blouse with puffy sleeves and a full-on swirly miniskirt. Somehow it crossed cheerleader with poodle to make ...

... 'a choodle?' Megan ventured.

Finally, Amber teamed a vibrant pink top and cropped chocolate jacket with skinny blue trousers – just in case he picked her up on his motorbike.

'Perfect. You look wonderful,' Megan said. 'So where are you going?'

Amber's eyes glittered with excitement. 'I don't know, but I bet it'll be amazing.'

'I hope so, for your sake. Dylan didn't even turn up to our first date, because someone gave him tickets to a gig at the last minute! We laugh about it now, but I wasn't happy at the time.'

Amber applied a tiny smudge of green on her eyelids, to accentuate her emerald eyes. 'I still don't know why you're with Dylan,' she said.

'Oh, he's not too bad,' Megan said. 'Anyway, there's no such thing as the ideal boy, is there?'

Yes, there is, thought Amber, *and I'm getting ready to go on a date with him.*

Thomas took Andrea's hand and pulled her away from Ralph and his fascinating insects. He led her through a doorway onto a flat roof terrace that had spectacular views of the London skyline. There, they perched on the wall and laughed about Ralph.

'Only my mum could introduce me to someone that batty,' Andrea said.

Thomas took her hand. The touch of his warm skin made her feel uncomfortable. She snatched her hand away and asked, 'Er, what are you doing here, anyway?'

He lifted something out of the bag he was carrying. It was a box tied with ribbon, a present. 'I wanted to give you this.'

Andrea's face lit up when she saw that it was a limited-edition book on architecture. 'This is the book I need for my essay! How did you know?' She paused, then added softly, 'How do you manage to do all the strange and wonderful things you do?'

He looked her straight in the eye. 'Deep down, you already know the answer to that question,' he replied.

No, I don't, she thought, looking away. *I have no idea of who you are or why you're here.* She gazed thoughtfully at the spires and skyscrapers in the distance.

Soon she was telling him about her childhood. 'I was only nine years old, but I preferred painting to playing,' she said. 'I was pretty good, I guess, because Mum started organizing shows for me. Exhibitions of my "work", aged nine! I became known as 'the little prodigy' and my paintings were selling before I'd even finished them. The pressure was on to paint, paint, paint. And then I found that I wasn't enjoying it any more. So I stopped.

'I concentrated on my studies instead and I'm glad I did. I love learning. I haven't drawn anything since then . . . apart from one or two sketches.' She ran her hand over the cover of the book he had given her. 'I've never told anyone this before,' she whispered. 'It's my secret.'

His hand found hers again and their fingers entwined. There it was again, that warm feeling. 'Your secret is safe with me.'

Now what do I do? Kiss him? How do you kiss someone? She closed her eyes and leaned towards him, her lips tingling.

But at the last moment, he turned his face away from hers. 'I'm sorry, Andrea, I can't,' he said, getting up.

He left her standing on the roof terrace, in a state of confusion. *What did I do wrong?* she thought miserably. *Please make this feeling go away.*

Alice stood on the stage of the Brick Lane Theatre and went through the lines that she had fluffed earlier.

'What man art thou that, thus bescreened in night, so stumblest on my counsel. . .'

Why do I always fall over when I get to the bit about stumbling? she wondered, stepping awkwardly on an uneven floorboard and losing her balance.

What happened next defied the laws of time and space, she thought later, but suddenly Thomas was before her, shouting her name and catching her in his arms.

It took a few moments to catch her breath. 'What are you doing here? How did you find me?' she asked him, after he had gently put her down.

'I was looking for you. After what happened earlier, I thought you might be in need of a muffin. So I brought some along.'

They began talking about the rehearsal and how Edward had lost his temper. She voiced her fears that she should never have taken the part. It really belonged to Amber, after all. Soon the conversation moved on to her father and how bad she felt about lying to him.

'I don't know what I want any more,' she confessed. 'And now I've talked too much and bored you and you probably want to leave. . .'

They sat on the edge of the stage looking out at the empty auditorium. Just then, her tummy rumbled. Maybe it was the stage acoustics, or the noise was accentuated by the silence, but it sounded really loud. She felt absolutely mortified. It rumbled again. 'Um, by the way, that was my stomach.'

She caught his eye and they burst out laughing.

'I'd say it was time for these,' Thomas said, opening the box of muffins. 'Blueberry or chocolate?'

She didn't hesitate. 'Chocolate, yum!'

'You see? You instantly knew which one you wanted.'

'Why wouldn't I? It's a muffin.'

'But what if it were something more important?'

'That would be different.'

'It shouldn't be. When you let your heart decide, it's easy to make a decision.'

She thought about it while she munched on her muffin. 'If you're right,' she said hesitantly, 'and if I let my heart do the choosing. . .' She took a deep breath. 'Then I suppose it's not so hard to tell you that I want to be with you.'

There. She had finally said it. She smiled sweetly and leaned forward to kiss him, ready for the perfect moment with the perfect boy.

But he held her at arm's length. 'Alice,' he said sadly, looking into her blue eyes. 'I'm sorry. I can't.' He turned and walked away.

She felt herself falling like a stone into darkness. She fell deeper and further, darker and deeper, through doubt and despair, misery and defeat.

Later, when she finally landed with a soft bump on

her bed at home, her head came to rest on a pillow soaked with tears.

Make this feeling go away, she thought. *Please! It's the worst feeling ever.*

Amber was totally ready for Thomas when he rang the doorbell. It was time for her dreams to come true.

He chose me, she thought triumphantly, as he took her hand and led her along the street. OK, he hadn't come to pick her up on his motorbike . . . but never mind. Walking was romantic too!

'So, where are you taking me?' she asked.

'Where would you like to go?'

She shut her eyes and smiled. 'Somewhere I've never been before,' she said. *Take me to the moon*, she thought.

He grinned. 'Perfect, I know just the place,' he said as he led her down a side street. 'We're here!' he announced, standing in front of a red-brick building.

She looked up at the sign above the entrance. 'A nursery school?' she said.

'Yup.'

'But . . . what on earth? This isn't a date!' she spluttered angrily.

He laughed and took her hand. 'Just come with me,' he said.

She followed him inside the building. A little girl

was waiting by an open classroom door. 'Thomas!' she squealed when she saw him. Suddenly there was a crowd of little people gathered around him, all saying his name delightedly.

'Wait,' Amber said. 'They know you?'

Thomas nodded knelt down and smiled. 'Hello, everyone!'

'Are you going to read us a story?' one of the children asked, pronouncing the words with a cute lisp.

'Yes. . .' He stood up and put his arm around Amber. 'And today I brought a helper with me, too!'

'What?' Amber said.

Twenty minutes later, she was sitting cross-legged on the floor sewing dolls for a group of excited, demanding children, thankful that she could still remember how to do a running stitch and backstitch. She hadn't sewn since she was a child, when she would pinch fabric from her mum's workshop to play 'fashion' – she had forgotten how much fun it was. Her head filled with happy memories of creating outfits for her dolls and dressing-up box. *When did I forget this side of me?* she wondered.

All she ever did now was point to a photo in a magazine or catalogue and say, 'I want that.' But where was the satisfaction in that?

She held up a doll with brown wool hair and a purple dress. 'Who wants this one?'

'Me, me!' screeched a little boy, his face lighting up with joy as she handed it over.

'What are you going to call her?' she asked him.

'Amber,' he said. 'Because she's pretty.'

After a couple of hours, Thomas announced that it was time to leave.

'What'd you think?' he asked, when they were back on the street.

'It was a disaster!' she grumped. 'I was surrounded by kids shouting at me to make dolls non-stop, plus all their clothes and accessories, including a bowler hat! And I pricked myself with the needle ten times and—'

'So you liked it?' he interrupted.

She raised her fists in triumph. 'It rocked!' she yelled.

She smiled and turned to face him. 'Yes, I liked it – and I like you, too, even though I still don't know who you really are. . .' She let the words linger in the air. 'And now,' she said, leaning against an iron railing, 'I want a kiss!' She closed her eyes and moved her face towards his.

But instead of kissing her, he said, 'I'm sorry, Amber. I can't.'

He walked away leaving her reeling. *Rejected?* she thought. *But why?*

*

When football practice finished late that afternoon, Daniel had a word with Thomas. 'You played well, Anderson,' he said.

Thomas smiled. 'Thanks, captain.'

'Don't thank me – and stay away from my sister, understood?' Daniel said.

Thomas nodded obediently. 'Don't worry, you'll have nothing to worry about after today.'

Daniel was just about to ask him what he meant when Bill Martin shouted at the top of his voice, 'Hey everyone, Real Life is back!' In fact, Bill was so delighted that he ran into the hallway and started broadcasting his good news around the building.

There was instant pandemonium as people grabbed their phones and rejoined the social network. Thomas, too, went onto Real Life, where he posted three photos. Each was labelled with the names of the girls he had been with that afternoon – an architecture book for Andrea, a rag doll for Amber and the interior of the Brick Lane Theatre for Alice.

Back in her bedroom, feeling angry and confused, Amber was pouring out her heart to Megan when she saw the photos. 'So he went out with Tanaka and Keats as well!' she said with a gasp. 'I knew it! I hate them!'

Did he kiss them? she wondered.

*

Alice was outside the house slamming a ball against a wall when Daniel brought her phone to her. 'You dropped this on the stairs,' he said. 'Are you OK?'

'Whatever,' she replied miserably.

'It's Anderson, isn't it?' he said.

Just then, she saw the photos and fell against him, sobbing.

Andrea couldn't focus on her work, she couldn't concentrate on anything. Why hadn't Thomas kissed her? She couldn't work it out. Then she saw the photos.

She instantly regretted telling him her secrets. *I've been so stupid!* she thought. *I just want things to go back to how they were before, but how can they?*

She went straight to her phone and deleted Amber and Alice's contact details.

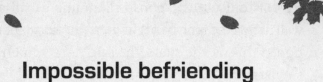

Impossible befriending

Life moves fast when you're at school. Nothing stays the same for long. Two days later, all anyone on Real Life could speak about was the field trip to the Natural History Museum.

LIZ LAPILLE
Amber deleted Edward from her friends!!!!

HELEN MASON
So? Weren't they already broken up?

SONJA CONSTANZA
So is Lynn queen bee now?

BRITNEY STATON
Lynn, what are you wearing tomorrow? Let's coordinate!

SONJA CONSTANZA

I heard Jess is going out with Daniel Keats now.

BRITNEY STATON

It's only a matter of time before Lynn and Edward get together, then.

MARKUS MULLER

Did you see Thomas throw Daniel Keats into the T. rex?

RODNEY LEE

Hahahahahah! I nearly died laughing! Sorry, Keats!

DANIEL KEATS

Whatever, so long as he stays away from my sister!

JAMES COLLINS

So, who *is* good enough for your sister?

DANIEL KEATS

Not you!

JAMES COLLINS

That's funny. I saw you having a stand-up argument with her!

That's what brothers and sisters do, dumbo!

Talking about arguments, did anyone see Edward
and Thomas shouting at each other?

I bet I know who that was about!

The only three people not joining in were still trying to work out what had happened at a secret meeting that nobody else knew about. It had not gone quite as expected. It all began with a text message that was sent to each of them at the same time, 12.30 p.m.

I'm sorry that I didn't reply to your
messages. I have so many things to
tell you. Let's meet in the Rainforest
Room and I'll explain everything. It's
not open to the public, but you can
still get in through one of the doors. ♥

The three girls made their way towards the closed-off area of the museum, their hearts singing. Each in turn found the Rainforest Room at the far end of a long, deserted corridor. Alice was imagining an afternoon of laughter. They would recite Shakespeare together. Andrea was looking forward to the feel of Thomas's fingers entwined in hers. They would talk about all the joint projects they planned to work on. Amber just wanted to dance with him. Then they would be together forever and everybody would realize that the queen had found her new king.

Happily ever after. The end.

One by one they found a door with 'Access Forbidden' written on it. Only Andrea hesitated before she went through it, knowing that she shouldn't be straying into an out-of-bounds area, far away from the rest of the school party. But, she decided, it was worth breaking the rules for love.

Wait, she thought, laughing silently to herself. *Had she, Andrea Tanaka, just decided that feelings were more important than law and order?*

She opened the door and stepped inside the Rainforest Room, which was filled with tropical trees and plants. Her heart beat rapidly as she wandered along a high walkway. Hearing a noise, she whipped around. Thomas? No, it was just the plip-plip of water dropping into a swampy pool far beneath her.

She walked slowly on and turned a corner, where to her surprise she saw Alice leaning on a rail.

'What are you doing here?'

Alice was equally astonished. 'What are *you* doing here?' she asked back.

'*No!* What are you two doing here?' Amber appeared from behind some palm trees.

Confusion turned to disappointment and anger as they realized that Thomas wasn't anywhere to be seen. Before long they were arguing about who should be there. No one was budging.

It was Alice who crumpled first, after Amber accused her of stealing her part in the play and Andrea called her a blonde stick insect. 'You know what? I don't want to be around you two for a second longer!' she screamed. She marched towards the door and yanked the handle, but the door refused to open.

'What's wrong? Forgotten how to open a door?' Amber sneered.

'It's stuck,' Alice said, feeling confused again.

Amber pushed her out of the way. But when she tried the door, the handle came off in her hand. 'Hmm, we have a problem,' she said.

'Who's the walking disaster zone now?' Andrea chipped in.

Alice started banging on the door and shouting for help – until Amber pointed out that no one would hear them so far away from the main museum area. 'But I have my mobile and I know how to use it,' she said.

There was no phone reception in the Rainforest Room, however. There was no way to get help. They were trapped.

'Does that mean I'm stuck with you two losers – again?' Amber said. 'This is unbearable! Ever since I met you, Keats, my life has become an endless series of problems!' she lashed out. 'And every time I run into you, Tanaka, something horrible happens! Plus, it's your fault I didn't get to kiss Thomas,' she roared.

'You didn't kiss Thomas?' Andrea asked.

'Hey, neither did I!' Alice said. 'Did you?'

'No,' Andrea said. 'Although I'm still not sure why. . .'

Amber laughed. 'I'll tell you why, Miss Never-Been-Kissed! Because you're the school nerd with a computer for a brain! No one wants to get a percentage rating for a kiss!'

'What did you say?' Andrea leaped on Amber, knocking Alice over in the process. Alice's bag fell off her shoulder, bounced and dropped off the side of the walkway.

Alice watched in horror. 'I hate you!' she shrieked. Hot tears poured from her eyes.

'Shhh!' Andrea said. 'What was that?' They heard a loud creaking coming from below.

'The walkway . . . is . . . moving?'

'Argh, the planks are splitting!'

The floor beneath their feet began to break into huge splintery segments. They flailed around in panic, desperately trying to find something to grasp onto – a rail, a wooden post – but there was nothing to cling to and they slipped through the gaps and plunged into the pool below. Luckily, the water, although suspiciously murky, was deep and warm.

It could have been so much worse. They could have been seriously hurt. But none of them thought about that as they came up for air.

Andrea emerged first, with Alice's bag around her neck, followed by Amber, who scrambled up onto a jetty and started walking away.

'Going to find Thomas?' Andrea asked, climbing up after her.

'What's it to you? He didn't kiss you, did he?'

'He didn't kiss you, either.'

Alice surfaced – her long blonde hair clinging to her face like seaweed – with a green bulgy-eyed lump on top of her head. 'Please tell me it's not a frog!' she wailed. The offending creature gave a loud croak and jumped back into the water. 'Ugh, gross!' Alice cried out, clambering out of the water as quickly as she could.

Amber burst out laughing. 'You look ridiculous!' she crowed.

Alice frowned and looked up at her. 'Look who's

talking,' she said, breaking into a wide grin. 'Your hair's as flat as a pancake, ha ha!'

Even Andrea was smiling. 'The whole thing is insane,' she said.

'We're all here because of a boy who doesn't even want us.'

'Speak for yourself,' Amber snapped, smoothing back her dripping hair. 'He wants me, I know it.'

'Oh, grow up and get real, Amber. He's just playing with us all,' Andrea said. 'Isn't that obvious by now?'

There was silence in the Rainforest Room as they absorbed Andrea's words. She was right. Thomas had made a fool of them all. Which was kind of comforting, in a way. At least he hadn't chosen one above the others.

Alice was the first to speak. 'This'll make you laugh. I made him a chocolate cake.' She pulled a soggy cardboard box out of her bag and threw it back into the pool. 'The piranhas can have it now.'

'I got him a book,' Andrea said ruefully.

Amber held up the scarf she had made him and they all collapsed into giggles.

'Does it mean that he's not our ideal boy, after all?' asked Alice.

'Maybe it means that even the perfect boy isn't worth it,' Andrea said.

Alice sat down on the jetty. 'He'll always be my idea

of perfection,' she said with a sigh. 'He's just how I imagined the perfect boy to be.'

'And me,' said Amber. 'It's incredible to think we dreamed him up in the library that day.'

'That's why I want to know who he really is,' Andrea said. 'Why would he come to us, only to reject us?'

'I know, it's weird, and we have to find out,' Amber said. 'But first, let's figure out a way to get out of here, because it looks like no one's coming to save us.'

It was Andrea who spotted the small window high up the wall a few moments later, and Alice who volunteered to climb through it. Andrea and Amber gave her a leg up and she hauled herself the rest of the way, yelping as she disappeared through to the other side.

'Are you OK?' Amber shouted.

She didn't reply.

'Alice!'

'Worried?' Alice said, opening the door and popping her head out. 'I didn't know you cared.'

'What about the jammed lock?'

Alice grinned. 'That's the funny thing – it just opened without me having to force it.'

'Quick,' we'd better hurry to get the bus,' Andrea said.

But Amber headed straight to the bathroom. She wasn't going anywhere without getting cleaned up first. No one was allowed to see her looking like a drowned rat! Except her new friends, that was. Alice and Andrea went with her and sat with her on the bus back to school.

Alice couldn't stop smiling. She had friends! She wasn't alone any more.

And soon everyone else knew it too when Amber, Andrea and Alice reconnected on Real Life.

That night, Thomas sat on his doorstep feeling pleased with himself. *Job done*, he thought, turning off his phone. Otto, his dog, came bounding up.

'Hello, boy!' Thomas said, throwing his arms around Otto's neck.

'Adam?' someone called. He turned round and saw a woman standing in the empty street, her hands dug into her coat pockets, a look of deep concern on her face.

'You must have the wrong person,' he said. 'My name is Thomas.'

'Yes, Rachel told me,' the woman replied. 'She also said I shouldn't come, but I needed to warn you.'

'Warn me? I don't understand.'

'The three girls,' she said. 'It's happening again, the same way it did before. . .'

'Before?'

'Don't make the same mistakes, or the consequences

will be terrible,' came the ominous reply. The woman swiftly turned and began to walk away.

'Who are you?' Thomas called after her.

'My name is Kathleen,' she said. 'Don't forget what I've said. Please, Adam, don't forget.'

Oh no, my parents!

It was Parent and Teacher Day at London International High School and everywhere there were students dutifully leading their parents from classroom to classroom for teacher meetings. Anticipation and dread filled the air.

Bill Martin's father entered the building with high expectations. He was looking forward to hearing the teachers praise his brilliant son. Bill had told him that he was a huge success at school, one of the most popular students and a hit with the girls.

'I'm really happy to be here,' said Mr Martin, beaming delightedly.

'Hi Amber!' Bill called out as the ex-queen bee walked past with her mother. Amber ignored him, and when he greeted Edward, the only reply was a mumble.

'Your classmates seem really unfriendly,' his dad said.

'Oh no, everybody loves me,' Bill said.

Alice bounced up and said, 'Hi, Bill!' with such enthusiasm that Mr Martin changed his mind. 'I'd like to introduce you to my mum,' Alice went on. She started burbling something to Bill, and Mrs Keats and Mr Martin were soon deep in conversation.

'Why so affectionate, dear?' Bill whispered.

'I need to distract my mum for the next four hours!' Alice replied. The one thing she could not let her mother do was talk to the drama teacher, who would no doubt praise Alice's commitment to the end-of-year show. Her mother knew almost nothing about the play! She certainly had no idea that Alice had skipped, or been late to, volleyball practice several times so that she could rehearse *Romeo and Juliet*.

As she led her mother off to meet the history teacher, she nearly had a panic attack when she saw a poster on the wall reminding students that play rehearsals were now taking place every day. She had told her dad it was only once a week! 'Over here,' she said, guiding her mum in the opposite direction.

'Don't you know your way around your own school?' her mother said with a laugh. She stopped to smooth a few loose strands of hair away from her daughter's face. 'You'd look so much better if you stood up straight,' she said.

Alice sighed inwardly. *This is going to be a very long day*, she thought.

Andrea's mother wasn't particularly interested in meeting her daughter's teachers. After years of being told that Andrea was the ideal student and a delight to teach, she knew what they were going to say before they even opened their mouths. 'But at least I'll get to meet your boyfriend again,' she said. 'Thomas, isn't it? He looked very cute, dear.'

'Mum, I don't think this is a good time to introduce you,' Andrea said.

Her mother looked genuinely upset. 'Why not? Are you ashamed of me?'

'Of course not, but the fact is, things aren't. . .'

Her mother put an arm around her. 'Sorry, sweetie, I'm forgetting how shy you are when it comes to matters of the heart. But you can confide in me, my darling, you know you can.'

Andrea tried leading her off to the chemistry room, but she wasn't going to be diverted. 'OK, I'll talk to your boring teachers, but afterwards I want to meet Thomas,' she said firmly.

Andrea sent out a distress signal to Amber and Alice.

ANDREA TANAKA
Have you seen Thomas?

AMBER LEE THOMPSON

No! And I don't want to.

ANDREA TANAKA

But he needs to pretend to be my boyfriend,
or my mother will never let it go!

ALICE KEATS

Are you really going to ask him after
what he did to us?

ANDREA TANAKA

Yes, if it will calm my mother
down!

ALICE KEATS

I can't help you, I have bigger problems!

AMBER LEE THOMPSON

Drop it, Keats. You don't have problems.
You're the darling of your family, more
mollycoddled than any of us.

ALICE KEATS

That's the problem!

*

Amber's mother instantly noticed a coolness in the air. 'Is it just me, or is no one saying hello to you today?' she asked her daughter.

Amber shrugged. 'Everyone's focused on the meetings, I guess.'

Her mum kept pressing. 'Darling, if there was something going on, you'd tell me, wouldn't you?'

'Stop it, Mum, you're being paranoid!' Amber snapped.

Her mother stepped forward and lightly touched her on the arm. 'I'm just trying to talk to you.'

'Well, stop,' Amber said.

'Why are you always like this?' her mother asked, unable to disguise the frustration in her voice.

Just then, Lynn ambled past. 'Fighting with your mum now, too?' she said cattily.

'Go somewhere you're wanted, Lynn,' Amber said.

Lynn clutched her heart. 'Ouch!'

'Now I know something's wrong,' Amber's mother insisted. 'Lynn is one of your best friends. Have you had a fight?'

Amber hung her head. 'Yes, Mum.'

'It can help to confide in your parents, darling,' her mother said gently.

Amber frowned and looked away. 'I'll talk to Dad, then. He understands me.'

'Amber—'

She sensed that her mother was about to say something important, but right at that moment Thomas walked by. 'I have to go,' she said. 'See you later, Mum.'

She immediately messaged Andrea, but by the time Andrea got back to her, Thomas had disappeared.

ANDREA TANAKA
Strange, he almost never does that!

*

Alice was waiting glumly for her mother outside the maths room when James came up. 'So you're not enjoying yourself, either?' he said.

'Not much.' She sighed. She couldn't be bothered with James. At the Natural History Museum, he had made fun of her for going on a date with Thomas and she had decided that he was really mean-hearted.

But he seemed to be in a different mood today. Was he actually trying to be nice to her?

'So why don't you leave your mum with your brother for a bit?' he suggested. 'Doesn't she need to meet his teachers, too?'

'Daniel's at football practice,' she explained wearily, 'and nothing's more important to Mum than practice.'

'You could ask him to come here when he's finished.'

'I could,' she agreed, 'if we were on speaking terms.' She put her head in her hands and turned away from him. 'Just two more meetings before we see the drama teacher,' she groaned.

James was puzzled. 'What's the problem? Mr O'Neill is the nicest guy and all he'll say is that you're fantastic and talented, because it's true.'

She finally looked at him. 'You really think so?'

'Yeah, but don't let it go to your head,' he said.

'You don't understand,' she said, and then it all came tumbling out – how important volleyball was to her family, how she had promised not to neglect it, how she had lied to her father about how often she was going to rehearsals. 'I'm always late to practice and until now my teammates have covered for me, but Dad is getting suspicious.' She closed her eyes. 'I just don't know what to do.'

'Just tell your dad!' he advised her. 'He seems like a good guy, not too strict.'

'He's lovely,' she said. 'I just don't want to disappoint him – or my mum.'

Her mother appeared. 'It's English next, is it?' she said, giving James a polite smile.

'I have to go. Thanks for listening to me,' Alice said to him.

'No problem,' he replied dismissively, 'I guess I didn't have anything better to do.'

Was I right? she thought. *Have you got a mean heart? Or were you actually being all right to me for a moment, back then?*

Jay outright refused to pretend to be Andrea's boyfriend. 'I'm sorry, I have things to do,' he said coolly.

'But, Jay, I really need—'

'I said I can't.'

She was stunned. What was the matter with him? As he packed up his books in silence and left the study room, she realized that he hadn't spoken to her in days, since the museum trip. Had she done something to upset him?

She looked at her watch. Any moment now her mother would be coming out of her last teacher meeting, expecting to meet Thomas. But there was no Thomas – and no Jay to stand in for him. What was she going to do?

Just along the corridor, Amber's mother was trying hard to get through to her daughter. 'Amber, I know that sometimes we've—'

'Ivy Lee Thompson!' a voice called out. Amber looked up and saw Andrea's mum rushing towards them, waving her arms.

Amber's mum smiled. 'Joelle! How many years has it been?'

'Too many!' called Alice's mum, coming to join them.

'Emily Keats!' the others shrieked. 'You haven't changed a bit!'

Amber scowled. 'Since when did you three know each other?'

'Since always!' her mother said excitedly. She turned away to carry on chatting.

'Great, an old girls' reunion,' Amber mumbled, walking off. She got out her phone and posted a wish on Real Life.

AMBER LEE THOMPSON
Make this day end quickly!

Meanwhile, Alice was hiding in a broom cupboard, hoping her mother wouldn't notice until it was too late to see the drama teacher.

ALICE KEATS
How long can I stay in here before she sends out the search squad?

In a state of utter panic, Andrea was pleading with everyone on Real Life to send her a fake boyfriend.

ANDREA TANAKA
Anyone will do!!!

Anyone? Uh-oh.

'Hey there, sweetcakes!'

Andrea whirled round. Bill was standing behind her, a messy, dishevelled wreck, his hair standing on end. She couldn't help laughing. Not Bill, surely?

'What happened to your hair?'

He hastily smoothed it with his hands. 'My dad ruffled it up when he was, er, expressing his dissatisfaction with me,' he explained. 'He messed my clothes around too.'

'He got annoyed, huh?'

'Maybe I slightly exaggerated my status within these walls,' Bill said.

'You almost never do that, do you?'

He laughed. 'Can I help it if I'm the funniest person in school?'

How far can I take this without giving him a kick? Andrea thought. 'I almost agree with you,' she said with a smile.

He lunged forward, lips puckered up. 'You can give me a kiss if you like.'

Ugh. 'No,' she said politely. 'But you can be my boyfriend.'

'Huh?' he said.

'Come with me, I have a plan,' she said, taking his hand and leading him away.

Amber learned a lot of interesting things as she listened idly to her mother chatting to Emily Keats and Joelle Tanaka. For instance, Andrea's mother was talking about Andrea's boyfriend. Like, what? Next she was saying that Andrea was a really talented artist. Oh yeah, since when?

Alice's mother started explaining how volleyball meant the world to her daughter. Amber laughed to herself. So she wasn't the only one who didn't communicate with her mum, then!

'Do you know where Alice is?' Emily Keats asked Amber.

'Sure, follow me.' Amber led Emily to the broom cupboard where Alice was hiding. She opened the door to reveal Alice standing gormlessly among a load of cleaning supplies.

'Good heavens, Alice, what on earth are you doing in there?' her mother asked.

'Hi Mum, there you are!' Alice said brightly, as if it

was perfectly normal to stand around in cupboards. 'Nothing, I was just. . .'

'Come here,' her mum interrupted. 'Stand up straight and let's go. There won't be time to see your drama teacher if we don't hurry.'

'That's what I was hoping,' Alice whispered to Amber as Emily dragged her away.

'It's going to take a miracle to get you out of this mess,' Amber said with a laugh.

As if by magic, Daniel appeared in the hallway, wearing his football kit. He was limping and rubbing his head.

'What are you doing here, darling?' Emily Keats asked worriedly. 'Shouldn't you be at practice?'

'Mum, I need to go home,' he said, rubbing his head again. 'I don't feel well.'

She rushed over to him. 'Why? What is it? What happened?'

'I just need to go!' Daniel insisted.

'But what about Mr O'Neill?'

'He'll get over it, Mum. It's only drama class, after all.' Daniel reached down and touched his knee. 'Ow!' he cried.

'Is it OK with you if I go, Alice?' her mother asked. 'Will you apologize to Mr O'Neill for me?'

Alice swallowed her shock and tried her best to sound casual. 'Sure, Mum! As Dan says, it's only drama! Go – and don't worry at all. Hope you feel better, Dan.'

I can't believe it, she thought, as they walked away.

Daniel turned back and winked at her. 'Truce, OK?' he mouthed.

When they were safely out of sight, Amber burst into fits of laughter. 'You wanted a miracle. You got one.'

Alice was leaning against a wall for support. 'I'm speechless.'

'You could try saying thank you,' James said, ambling towards them.

'Why?' Alice asked.

'A little bird must have told Daniel his sister needed help. . .' he said, sounding pleased with himself.

'You're the little bird?' Alice asked with disbelief.

'Yup, but there's no need to go all starry-eyed about it,' he said with an embarrassed laugh. 'I like to make myself useful occasionally, that's all.'

'Well, thank you!' she said.

'No problem,' he murmured.

Amber led Alice away. 'Nice one, Keats. Maybe you're not such a disaster with boys, after all,' she said. 'Anyway, forget boys and come with me. I want to show you something.'

Alice was amazed when she saw Amber's costume designs for *Romeo and Juliet* in the theatre dressing room. 'Did you really draw these?' she asked her for the third time. 'They're so, so beautiful.'

'You think?' Amber asked.

'Out of this world!' She pointed to the sketch of a full-length, halter-neck silk dress. 'But could you actually make something like that?'

Amber opened a drawer. 'You know ... well ... I gave it a try...' She pulled out a lilac silk dress that matched the design exactly. 'Is it terrible?'

Alice snatched it from her and hugged it against her body. 'You made this? It's amazing! Wow, you're really talented, Amber!'

Amber looked into the middle distance. 'Yes, I think so too,' she said airily.

'It's perfect. You have to design the costumes for the play!'

'I'd like to, but I can't see Edward allowing it.'

They both knew it was a long shot, but nothing was impossible. Lynn had pulled out of designing the costumes after the museum trip and Edward hadn't found anyone to replace her yet. He might not like the idea of Amber taking over, but what choice did he have?

'Plus, it will all be free if I use leftover fabrics from my mum's studio,' Amber added.

'Edward won't be able to say no and you'll be back in the show!' Alice said.

They clasped hands. 'I like the way you think, Keats,' Amber said. 'Ready to go onstage? It's time for rehearsal.'

While Alice gazed up at Thomas, her Romeo, as he went through a scene onstage, Amber messaged Andrea to say they had found him.

ANDREA TANAKA
Thanks, but I don't need him any more.

'Neither do we, right, Alice?' Amber said.

But Alice was lost in a dream of remembering all the good experiences she'd had with Thomas: that first moment she saw him in the rain on the school steps; the time they recited Romeo and Juliet's lines to each other outside; and their precious hour together at the Brick Lane Theatre, when he had told her to follow her heart.

Amber snapped her fingers in front of her face. 'He made fun of us!' she reminded Alice.

Alice sighed dejectedly. 'I know. But how can we play star-crossed lovers when Romeo doesn't actually love Juliet?'

'Er, you're acting, remember?' Amber said.

Thomas didn't even look Alice's way as she approached the stage. She wondered what he was thinking. Maybe he was just concentrating on his lines. Perhaps he had already forgotten their moments together. Either way—

'Hey, look where you're going!' yelled one of the stage hands.

She tripped over a light stand, flew through the air and landed with a *rippp*.

I've really torn it now, she thought, inspecting the huge tear in her sack dress.

Vanessa Austin snapped a picture. Vanessa had recently become one of Lynn's little sidekicks – and Lynn had told her to post anything that would make Amber or her new friends look stupid. This was perfect!

'Cut it out, Vanessa,' Amber said, pushing past her. 'Alice Keats's #embarrassingmoments aren't funny any more.'

Vanessa's eyes narrowed. 'Oh yeah? Who says?'

Amber held her gaze. 'I say.' She made her way up to the stage. 'Don't worry, Alice, I'll fix your dress now.' Kneeling at Alice's feet, she began to measure the rip and pin it back together.

Vanessa took a photo of her and posted it on Real
Life.

VANESSA AUSTIN
The ex-queen is on her knees.

Onstage, Amber's phone alerted her to the photo
and comment, but she barely registered it. Within a
couple of minutes, a conversation had started about
the meaning of Vanessa's post.

MAY RODRIGUEZ
Surprise, surprise, it turns out that
Thompson knows what friendship
is.

LYNN JAVINS
Ha, don't be fooled!

MAY RODRIGUEZ
Don't be jealous, Lynn!

LYNN JAVINS
Come on, she's on her knees to
Alice Keats. Humiliation central!

When Amber had finished her repairs, not only was the tear invisible, but Alice's dress now had a beautiful brocade border. The rest of the cast gathered round to admire her work.

Edward arrived to find the cast passing round Amber's costume designs. 'What's this?' he said angrily, snatching a sheaf of paper from one of the actors.

'You have to see Amber's designs, they're amazing!'

'I'll see them when I want to,' he said. He ripped up the drawing and threw it away. 'I'm the director. I say who designs my costumes, no one else.'

He glared at Amber and she glared back.

'At least look at them,' Alice protested.

He turned to Alice. 'I didn't ask for your opinion, Keats. Since when were you a fashion expert?'

She felt herself faltering, but willed herself to stand up for her friend. 'It's just that . . . they're really beautiful . . . and I think, er, Amber would be . . . a brilliant costume designer for our show.'

There. She'd said it. 'Oh, and, er . . . everyone else thinks so too.'

The nods and murmurs that followed this statement told Edward all he needed to know.

'Well, Amber,' Edward said, 'I see you have everybody's approval again. So you're our costume designer now, fine.'

'Great, thanks,' Amber mumbled, looking down.

'But don't start thinking you've beaten me,' he warned her softly. 'Because you haven't and you never will.'

In an empty maths classroom, Andrea was giving Bill a crash course in how to pretend to be her boyfriend – and he was loving every painful minute of it. 'Yes, sweetcakes,' he kept saying with a dreamy smile. 'Whatever you say.'

Andrea finally snapped when he called her 'sweetcakes' for the hundredth time.

'Never call me that again, OK, doughnut face? Never, never!' she burst out.

'OK,' he agreed meekly.

Then it was show time.

Out into the hallway they went, arm in yucky arm. There they found Andrea's mum, who was surprised to see her daughter cosying up to a boy who appeared to be the opposite of Thomas.

'He's your boyfriend?' she asked hesitantly.

'Yes,' Andrea said, as brightly as she could. Bill gave her a squeeze and told Joelle how pleased he was to meet the mother of his 'sweetcakes'.

Andrea's mother continued to look astonished. 'But. . . I'm sorry – and excuse me for asking this, Bill – what happened to Thomas?'

Andrea giggled. 'That's why I didn't want to tell you anything, you see. We broke up! And now I have Bill!' She made out that it was all so hilariously simple.

'Trust me, she couldn't do better,' Bill said, giving Joelle a nudge. He made kiss noises at Andrea and she pretended to find it cute. *Ugh.*

'Well, what can I say!' Joelle said. There was a note of doubt in her voice and she paused before adding anything. Then she smiled. 'All I care about is my girl's happiness. I just don't want you to be alone. I worry so much—'

'Too much,' Andrea said.

'I know, but you're my only daughter. . .'

'My poor lonely sweetcakes,' Bill said, going in for a hug. Andrea elbowed him away, hoping that it would look as if she was being 'playful'.

'Hey, now you've met Bill, you can relax!' she

told her mum. 'Can't you?' Bill tried to get close again and she shoved him away, harder this time.

'Of course, darling, of course!' her mother gushed.

Andrea had to get to the theatre for play rehearsals, so after telling Bill what a pleasure it had been to meet him, she made her way home.

'Did I do a good job?' Bill asked, when Joelle was out of sight.

'Yes, thank you,' Andrea said.

'Shall we do it for real next time?' he asked with a wink.

'I owe you a favour and then we're done,' she said diplomatically.

'Are you sure you don't want to go on a date?' he said.

She was about to run away as fast as she could when Bill's father came round the corner. 'Is this your girlfriend, son?' he asked with a chortle. 'Why, you old fox!'

'Debt repaid,' she whispered, as she smiled and said how nice it was to meet her boyfriend's dad at last. Bill had no choice but to nod his agreement.

Edward decided that they would rehearse the fight scene.

'But we've all prepared for the balcony scene,' Alice said.

Edward looked as if he was about to lose his temper again. 'I've already told you once, Keats. I make the decisions!'

'Fine, Eddie,' Thomas said. 'But since Romeo isn't in the fight scene, I'm going to football practice.'

'You're not going anywhere!' Edward roared.

Thomas was already on his way. 'And who's going to stop me, Eddie?' he asked.

'Eddie?' boomed a voice. 'Aha, so I'm not the only one who calls you that!' A grey-haired man in a suit stepped out of the shadows, instantly recognizable as an older, steelier version of Edward.

Edward stiffened. 'Dad?' he said. 'What are you doing here?'

Amber's heart went out to him, despite everything. She knew that Edward had a difficult relationship with his father. Although she had met Mr Bradford only a couple of times, it had been plain to see that he was always demanding the impossible of his family. He was often away on business and his work came first, yet he expected his wife and son to stand to attention whenever he appeared. Which was what Edward was doing right now.

'Head Teacher Barnes told me about your role as director, so I've come to see you at work,' Mr Bradford said. 'I'm surprised you didn't tell me about it, I must say.'

Edward looked uncomfortable. 'Well, we haven't seen each other much lately.'

His father laughed and said something to Mrs Barnes about having a business empire to attend to. 'But you could have emailed me, Eddie,' he bellowed.

'I did,' Edward said. 'To say that Grandma was in hospital.'

His father waved his hand dismissively. 'Oh, that. So you did.' He and Mrs Barnes sat down. 'Now let me see a little of what you're doing with this show, son.'

'Yes, sir,' Edward said.

'I want to see whether he's developing leadership qualities,' his father explained to Mrs Barnes.

'Oh, he most certainly is,' she assured him.

'Really? I would never have known. It just goes to show, doesn't it? Children are always different in their home environment. . .'

Onstage, a panicky Edward was trying to keep things together. 'Let's begin, everyone,' he said. 'Thomas, you're not leaving until we've finished!'

Thomas laughed. 'OK, Eddie.'

'Quiet!' Edward yelled.

'Son!' his father shouted from the auditorium. 'The first rule of leadership is never to raise your voice!'

Edward looked pained. 'I'm giving directions for the show, Dad, thanks,' he said through clenched teeth.

And then it came to him. A total brainwave.

'As you already know,' he told the cast, 'this is a minimalist interpretation of *Romeo and Juliet*, which means that it is completely new and different.'

'Here we go,' Alice whispered to Amber. 'He's really hamming it up for his dad.'

'A show where the set and script will be stripped to the bare minimum,' he went on. He motioned towards Alice. 'A show where the protagonist is mute!'

Alice felt like she'd been struck by a thunderbolt. 'What?' she said. 'Did I hear you right?'

Edward smiled. 'I said mute, not deaf, Keats – and you heard me. My Juliet will not speak!'

'Hey, you can't do that!' Amber yelled.

'That's enough!' he snapped. 'We've already lost too much time. Let's go!'

'Bravo!' called out his father. He turned to Mrs Barnes. 'For the first time, I feel I've invested well in this school.'

'Oh, thank you,' she said, hoping that another fat cheque would be on its way soon.

'Young lady, he certainly made things easier for you!' Mr Bradford told Alice with a chuckle. 'You won't have to tire yourself out learning your lines now.' He strode out of the theatre, wishing everyone luck.

Alice was close to tears. She bit her lip to stop herself from crying.

'Edward,' she said, 'you can't take all my lines away.'

He folded his arms. 'Too bad. I just did.'

She stayed silent, a flood of tears rolling down her cheeks.

'Oh well, nothing's happening today, clearly,' Thomas said. 'So I'm going to football practice.'

'Is that all you're going to say?' Amber asked him.

He looked surprised. 'What else is there?'

'Aren't you going to stick up for Alice?'

He shrugged. 'Why should I?' he asked, turning and walking away. 'I can't always be there for you all.'

Amber, Andrea and Alice were sitting on a bench in the school garden.

'He can't do it,' Amber said. 'It's way too crazy. A mute Juliet! He'll have to back down.'

'Edward back down? First the sky has to fall in,' Alice said.

The others knew what a disaster it was for Alice. If she had no lines in the play, she wouldn't be able to show her parents that she could act. And if they didn't see how well she could act, how could she persuade them that she was making the right choice in giving up volleyball?

Amber stood up. 'I promise you, we'll find a solution,' she vowed.

'But how?'

'I don't know I but we'll do it together,' Andrea said.

'And it'll rock!' Amber declared.

Alice wasn't sure what they had in mind or how on earth they would put it into action, but she felt grateful to have her friends with her in this moment of crisis.

'Thank you,' she said.

Thomas was in the computer room. A new message appeared on his screen.

KATHLEEN BENSON
You don't remember anything about 1989?

Kathleen? he thought. *The woman I met the other night outside my house?*

There was a photo attached to the message of two girls standing in front of the school. One was Rachel, the librarian, looking incredibly young.

The other woman was. . .? The handwritten note on the photograph identified her as Kathleen.

So they really do know each other, he thought. *But what does any of this have to do with me?*

He started searching the computer archives. There was nothing for 1989/90.

'Only paper archives?' he muttered. 'How did people survive in those days?'

At last he found the shelf reference for the yearbook he was looking for, and went to the library to find it. He was hoping it would shed light on the mystery surrounding Kathleen. Perhaps it would make her go away. The yearbook was just like any other. He flicked through the pages. Lots of smiling students. Then he stopped at a page featuring the best photography club photos. 'What on earth is—' he exclaimed.

There, in two of the photos, was a boy who looked just like him. In the first picture, he was standing between Kathleen and Rachel, the librarian. In the second, he was looking at a girl Thomas had never seen before. Underneath both photos, the caption identified his double as 'Adam Burton'.

'Who are you, Adam Burton?' Thomas asked aloud. 'Why do you look exactly like me?'

Operation Rockspeare

Feeling happier than she'd been in ages, Amber sat on the floor of her mother's design studio sewing costumes for the play. She was just finishing off the hem of a tunic when she heard a commotion outside the fitting rooms.

'I'm not wearing this!' shrieked one of the house models. She was standing in front of a mirror draped in a frumpy blue dress. 'It'll ruin my image!'

She had a point. 'Is that one of your designs?' she asked her mum.

Her mother made a face. 'No, I had to make it up from a sketch the client sent me.'

'Well, I refuse to wear it!' the model insisted.

'Don't worry, Chloe,' Ivy Lee Thompson soothed, moving towards her with a box of pins. 'I'll just do what I did with the green elephant.'

'What are you talking about, Mum?' Amber asked.

'Didn't I ever tell you that story?' her mother said. 'It was a very long time ago, when I was still a model.' She began to pin folds into Chloe's dress. 'I was doing a catwalk show for Chaneaux and I had to wear a horrible saggy dress that made me look like a green elephant. Since I couldn't bear to be seen in it, I modified it at the last minute using a length of a yellow ribbon to give it some shape – without telling the stylist.'

'What happened then?' Amber asked eagerly. 'Didn't the stylist get angry?'

'Very! But it was a huge hit and became the most popular dress in the collection, so he ended up having to congratulate me.'

Amber giggled. 'That's so cool!'

'Then he decided that I had a little talent and asked me to work with him,' her mum went on. 'So it's thanks to that green elephant dress that I became a stylist, which led me to designing. My point is that sometimes you need to be brave enough to step outside the box and see what happens. . .'

'Great story!' Amber said, going back to her sewing. 'Hey!' she said, after a few minutes, suddenly sitting up straight. 'Mum, you're a genius!' She quickly packed up her stuff and left the studio in a hurry, saying she would be back later.

Out on the street, she hailed a taxi while yelling into her phone. 'Andrea! I know what to do! The answer could not be simpler!'

*

Andrea was in the library browsing books. 'Are you sure?' she whispered when she heard what Amber was planning.

'We can do it!' Amber said with a whoop. 'Do me a favour – call Alice and tell her. I'll speak to you again on Real Life.'

In the taxi, she created a new group on Real Life – a closed group – and named it 'Rockspeare'. Back at school, in their PSHE class, she, Alice and Andrea started compiling a list of the people they needed to recruit to put Amber's idea into action.

'What are you doing?' Jess asked with a sneer. 'Making a list for the most boring party of the year?'

'Almost right,' Amber said with a smile. 'It's a list of the worst put-downs of the century and guess what? You're at the top!'

Mr Bailey, the teacher, cleared his throat. 'Now then, everyone,' he said, bringing a box of dolls out of the store cupboard. 'For the next assignment, you have to take care of these electronic babies. Each has a computer inside to record its status data. I'll assign your grades based on this data.'

The classroom fell silent.

'Is there one for each of us?' Bill asked eventually.

'No,' Mr Bailey replied, smiling. 'You'll be working in pairs – and I've already drawn up a list based on your compatibility.'

No one spoke. One thing was certain – old Bailey didn't have the slightest clue about his students' compatibility, as proved when he paired Andrea with Bill and Edward with Megan, who had just returned from her suspension. But then he put together Alice and James, who weren't exactly displeased to be paired. And, in the world according to Amber, he totally got it right when he matched her with Thomas . . . if only Thomas hadn't been absent.

'So, where is Anderson?' Mr Bailey asked.

He didn't get an answer, but Alice told Andrea that Thomas hadn't been in school for a while, and Andrea said that he seemed to have vanished entirely.

To Andrea's utter dismay – although she wasn't quite sure why it upset her so much – Jay was partnered with Amber in Thomas's absence. She must have shown it on her face, because Amber asked if she was OK.

'Hmm? Yes, fine!' she said brightly. But she had no idea what to say to Jay when he approached Amber – and he clearly felt the same way, because not a word passed between them.

Amber shoved her doll at Jay and ran off to catch up with Megan, 'I have so many things to tell you, but first I need to ask you something.' She began whispering excitedly into Megan's ear.

*

With Otto by his side, Thomas stood outside Kathleen's house in High Barnet and took a deep breath. *Here goes*, he thought, ringing her doorbell. There was no answer. After standing around for a few minutes, Otto grew impatient and pushed at the front door with his nose. It opened. Thomas walked inside, calling Kathleen's name. There was no one there.

He put his head round the door of the nearest room and was surprised to see a pinboard filled with photos, notes and newspaper cuttings. Some were recent. Others were dated 1989. It was the kind of display you saw in TV police programmes, where the detectives plotted out the clues and evidence of a crime. Moving closer, Thomas saw photos of Adam Burton, Rachel and Kathleen. Underneath Adam's photo was a note with the date of his birthday, 29 September. 'The same day as my birthday?' he whispered. 'It can't be.' He didn't like it one bit.

He read on, then stopped horrified. Adam had arrived at the school after a fire, just as he had – and had disappeared the day after a school trip to the Natural History Museum. Written on one

155

of the notes was a question: 'Why is Thomas still here?'

What does it mean? he wondered, feeling sick with confusion. *Who is Adam and who am I?*

By mid-morning, Real Life was backed up with cries for help from distressed 'parents' of electronic dolls.

MARKUS MULLER

Our doll has been wailing for half
an hour – what do we do?

RODNEY LEE

You're asking me? Mine hasn't shut
up for even a second.

BILL MARTIN

Neither has mine! Help me now,
or I'll go mad!

ALICE KEATS

Have you tried cuddling it?

BILL MARTIN

I've been cuddling it for half an hour!

Andrea was standing next to him and the

screaming doll, frantically reading a baby manual on her phone. 'Will you stop asking people for help?' she snapped. 'We can manage perfectly well by ourselves.'

'Oh yeah?' Bill said, his ears vibrating painfully as the baby's shrieks grew louder.

'It says here that it might need a change of nappy.' She sniffed the doll's bottom and nearly dropped it. 'Yuck!' The baby went straight back to Bill.

'Hypothesis correct!' she barked. 'Proceed with operation nappy change!'

Bill wasn't buying it, but Andrea sternly warned him that it was his duty as a co-parent to share the workload – and so he duly changed the nappy. The doll calmed down. All was quiet. They sighed with relief – and then the crazily awful sound of persistent bawling started up again.

'It's hungry,' Bill said. 'We need to prepare its bottle.'

'But what temperature should the milk be?' Andrea scrolled down the manual. 'Argh, there are pages and pages on the subject! Room temperature versus slightly warm ... bacteria ... infection...' Her mind started reeling.

'Wah wah wah!' cried the baby.

Andrea wiped her brow. 'I think I need a break from being a mum!'

Amber had other business. May, Sonja and Kim were waiting for her on a bench outside

'I've got a proposal for you. Listen up,' said Amber

Five minutes later, May, Sonja and Kim joined the *Rockspeare* group.

Alice and James were getting on fine with their baby. Alice was lost in thought while she cuddled it in her arms, James was deep into childcare research online. All was harmony, until James came up behind Alice and the baby, brandishing a bottle of milk. 'Here!' he said proudly.

'Whoa!' Startled, she jumped and let go of the doll.

'Careful, the baby!' James warned, as it dropped out of her arms. He dived forward and caught it just in time.

'I'm sorry!' she said, her hand flying to her mouth. 'That was typical of me.'

'No, problem. Disaster avoided.' He chuckled.

Her head drooped. 'Am I just a joke to you?'

'No, but you do make me laugh, Keats.' He started listing his favourites from her many #embarrassingmoments on Real Life. 'When you tipped your tray on the floor . . . that time you were carrying so many books it's was just obvious what was going to happen . . . the oil stain on your sports shirt. . .'

Where's my red nose and big shoes? she thought. *I'm just a clown.*

'Hey, don't take it the wrong way,' James said gently, his hand brushing hers. 'I like anyone who can make me laugh. Really.'

She looked into his hazel eyes and her head swam. *He's being nice now?*

While Bill and Andrea's milk boiled over for the second time, Jay was absolutely hating being a single parent.

How can Amber do this to me? he thought, resentment welling up as he changed his fifth nappy.

AMBER LEE THOMPSON
Nearly finished. I won't be long now.

Amber made her way to the theatre where three of the stage crew were fiercely concentrating on the job of connecting fuses to the control panel. She stood in the doorway, watching them. They were like a whole other species – the behind-the-scenes guys who scuttled around solving problems on set and never saw the light of day.

'Is it OK if I come in?' she called out.

'Who is she talking to?' one of them asked.

His friend shrugged. 'No idea. We're the only ones here.'

She stepped inside. 'Bruce, Alan, Eddie, right?'

Their mouths dropped open. 'She knows our names. What's going on?'

She flashed her most dazzling smile. 'Can I ask you a favour?'

'Us?'

Five minutes later, Bruce, Alan and Eddie joined the *Rockspeare* group.

Amber went to find Andrea, who was at her wit's end. The baby was crying and Bill was panicking – if looking after a baby really was this hard, then it was a mystery to both 'parents' how the human race had survived so long.

'Can't you make it stop?' Amber yelled with her fingers in her ears.

'I don't know how!' Andrea said in despair.

'Nothing's working!' Bill added helplessly.

Amber took Andrea's hand. 'Give Bill the baby and come with me.' She marched her out of the room into the hallway.

Andrea leaned against a wall. 'Phew, I needed a break.' She closed her eyes for a second.

'Hey, what's going on with you?' Amber asked.

'You'll understand one day, when you're a parent,' Andrea replied wearily.

Amber was impatient to move on. 'This baby thing has fried your brain. Can you just listen to what I have to say?'

'Go on,' Andrea said, slowly coming back to life.

'OK, here's the plan,' Amber said. 'We'll rehearse a different production, our own version of *Romeo and Juliet*.'

'Our own version?'

'Something more like the idea I had for a rock musical at the beginning of term, before Mrs Barnes shot it down for being too unconventional. Megan's going to write the music and I'll do the costumes.'

'How's it going to work? You'll have to substitute it for Edward's show right at the last minute – otherwise he'll block it.'

Amber's green eyes glistened. 'Exactly! It'll be too late to stop us if we're already onstage.'

'Interesting.'

'Alice will have her lines restored and she'll be able

to show her parents how great she is,' Amber went on.

'And you'll get your revenge on Edward...' Andrea gave her a mischievous look.

'Yes, maybe...' Amber thought about it. She would be lying if she said it wouldn't be satisfying to beat Edward at his own game, but was that what was driving her? 'Actually, it's not so much about that,' she said. 'I want this to be everybody's show, not just the director's.'

Andrea looked doubtful. 'Is that really true?'

'It is!' Amber said. 'And when I say I want it to be everybody's show, that includes you, too!'

'Me? You want to use my photos for the sets? Sure.'

Amber smirked. 'Not so fast, Brainy Boots! I want you to paint the sets for me.'

'Oh no,' Andrea said softly. 'Sorry, I don't paint.'

Amber folded her arms. 'Don't even try denying it, Tanaka. Your mum told me you were an amazing painter when you were little.'

'But that was when I was a kid!'

What followed next was not an argument, more of a negotiation. Amber needed a set painter. She had also clocked Andrea's unhappiness about the situation with Jay – and this was her bargaining chip. It was a happy coincidence that Jay was Amber's co-parent in the baby project.

'If you paint the *Rockspeare* sets, in return I can talk to Jay and help mend your friendship. . .'

Andrea's face lit up. 'Would you really do that?' she said. 'Not that I care that much,' she added quickly, trying to neutralise her expression. She hated showing her feelings. 'Although it's not easy when your best friend won't speak to you – and you don't even know why,' she added.

'I'll talk to him and find out what's wrong, OK?'

Andrea hesitated. 'OK, you win,' she said eventually.

Amber raised a triumphant fist. 'Yes!' she said. 'Get your paintbrushes ready, because this is going to be the best show ever!'

Megan was hostile to Edward from the very beginning of their joint assignment – and she didn't stop scowling at him all day. 'Hey, I don't want to fight!' Edward told her. 'Let's just focus on getting a good grade.'

She instantly felt irritated. 'That's all that matters to you, huh? Making a good impression? It's all about appearances with you, isn't it?'

Edward tried to dodge the bullets, but Megan had him within point blank range.

Bang! 'I know what you did to Amber! I know everything.'

Bang! 'You hurt my friend and I'll never forgive you for it.'

Bang! 'One day you'll wake up and realize you've made the biggest mistake of your life – and maybe then you'll begin to find out what love really is.'

Their baby cried, their baby wailed – and Edward developed a thumping headache.

Alice and James smiled into the baby basket, where their doll was quietly sleeping. 'Isn't he darling?' Alice said.

Oh no! she thought. *I'm being mushy. Boys hate that. James is probably going to be sick!*

But all he said was, 'Yes, it's really cute.' He lowered his voice to a whisper. 'And he's finally asleep.'

As they leaned over the basket, their hands touched by accident. The effect was electrifying. Alice snatched her arm away, took a step backwards and fell clumsily onto the floor, knocking over a bookcase. Books flew everywhere, the baby doll started to cry and James burst out laughing.

'You really are a disaster, Alice,' he said, putting his arm out to help her up. 'It can't be easy being you.'

'It isn't,' she said, taking his hand.

Just then, Edward appeared in the doorway. 'Aw, cute,' he cooed sarcastically.

The smile left James's face. 'Ed! What are you doing here.'

'I need you.'

'But—' James looked at Alice.

'Come on, she can manage on her own.' He stopped, raising one eyebrow. 'Unless you'd prefer to stay with her?'

'You're joking?' James's voice took on a harsh tone. 'With Disaster Keats? No thank you!'

After he'd left, Alice sat slumped in a chair, the crying baby in her arms. 'Oh, what did you expect?' she asked the doll. 'Didn't I say he had a mean heart?'

Amber had one last thing to do – find Thomas. She messaged him, but he didn't get back to her.

Sorry, Amber, he thought as he jogged home with Otto. *I have other things to do, like find out why I'm still here!*

Otto started barking just before they reached the bookstore. 'What's wrong, boy?' Thomas asked him. He went to open the shop door, but it wouldn't budge. He looked through the window. The store was completely empty. He rattled the door again. 'Open up!' he yelled.

'No point shouting,' said a passer-by. 'That shop's been closed for fifteen years now, maybe more.'

'What do you mean, fifteen years?' Thomas said. 'It was open when I left here this morning.'

He ran off, with Otto bounding along beside him.

When he reached his uncle's warehouse in Chinatown, that was empty too.

'What's going on, boy?' he cried out. 'What's happening to me?'

Amber finally made it back to Jay, who was brimming with anger by the time she arrived. 'Where have you been?' he asked. 'Having a doll is your responsibility too! I didn't ask to do this on my own.'

'This assignment has really sent you over the edge, huh?' she said. 'Sorry, I had to meet Andrea...' She looked over at him to see how he would react to the mention of his best friend's name.

'Andrea?' he said, obviously startled. 'Hey, why are you staring at me like that?'

'Well, why are you so surprised to hear her name? And why are you angry with her?'

He shrugged, as if it was nothing at all – and suddenly she knew exactly what was going on. 'No way, Jay, you can't be in love with your best friend!' she burst out.

'What are you talking about?' he asked, laughing nervously.

She walked over to him with a smile on her face and placed her hands firmly on his shoulders. It was time for them to have a serious talk.

*

At the end of the day, the PSHE class regrouped in front of Mr Bailey. Amber was looking forward to a heap of praise, thanks to Jay's efforts with their doll. Andrea, on the other hand, was dreading her first ever fail. Megan and Edward didn't care; they just wanted to get away from each other.

Mr Bailey seemed pleased with everyone. 'In particular, I'd like to congratulate James and Alice,' he said. 'Please come to the blackboard, you two.'

Alice got up from her desk. 'James isn't here, I'm—'

'Here I am!' James appeared at the classroom door. 'Sorry to be late,' he said to Mr Bailey. Then he smiled at Alice, his hazel eyes sparkling with warmth. 'And sorry for everything else,' he added, putting his arms around her waist.

Alice's heart lurched and it felt like a hundred butterflies had just been set free inside her stomach.

Mr Bailey announced that he was giving Alice and James an A grade. 'As for everyone else ... we'll pretend none of this ever happened – although we will be discussing it tomorrow. You may go.'

No F grade! Andrea leaped up with happiness and nearly fell off her chair.

Jay rushed forward and caught her in the nick of time. 'Careful,' he said.

'Oops, sorry,' she said. 'Hey thanks,' she added, when she saw it was him.

He looked down. 'No problem.'

Were they friends again? 'Shall we go for a vegan burger at Joe's after school?' she asked.

'No, I can't,' he said, and left the classroom moments later.

She wilted. So they still weren't friends – why not? She was starting to miss him badly. Amber came up behind her. 'Give him time,' she said softly. 'He really cares about you, but. . .'

'But?'

'He needs to know you care about him too. So show him.'

'OK,' Andrea said, wondering how on earth she was going to do that.

Megan came over, finally free of Edward. 'How are the preparations going?' she asked eagerly.

Amber grinned. 'Everyone said yes,' she said in a low voice, conscious that Lynn and Jess were hovering nearby. 'Operation *Rockspeare* has officially started!' Megan whooped her approval.

They agreed to meet later to discuss the details over milkshakes in Best Shake at Hyde Park Corner.

Inside the cafe, Andrea, Amber and Megan talked excitedly about how brilliant *Rockspeare* could be if they could pull it off behind Edward's back. Alice arrived on her bicycle. 'Our leading lady!' Amber called out. 'How does it feel to be given your voice back?'

Alice hugged her gratefully. She had been walking around in a cloud of happiness since James had hugged her. Now she was meeting her friends to discuss their secret show. It was hard to believe how much her life had changed – and, to celebrate, she ordered a slice of cheesecake and a strawberry shake.

But, being Alice, she couldn't help worrying too. 'I don't want you to risk everything just for me,' she told Amber, as she waited for her order to come.

Amber gave her a friendly push. 'It's not just for you, it's for everybody. We'll all be able to show off our hidden talents,' she said. She was smiling, but then her expression grew serious. 'First we've got to work out where to rehearse, though, and—'

'I can't help,' Megan said, throwing her hands up. 'Dylan just had a fight with the owner of the garage where the Sad Cats rehearse, so I've already run out of ideas.'

'And then there's Thomas – Romeo – whatever,' Amber went on. 'Where is he? Assuming we even find him, how are we going to persuade him to join us?'

Alice's order arrived moments later. But as she picked up her strawberry shake, it slipped out of her hand and fell onto the table, spraying pink gloop in Megan's direction.

She was horrified. 'I'm so sorry!' she said, grabbing a handful of paper towels. 'So, so, sorry!'

Megan looked down at her top, which was soaking wet. 'Don't worry,' she said. 'I don't care about the T-shirt, but I should get going: I'm allergic to strawberries.' She got up to leave. 'I can feel myself getting itchy already,' she added with a giggle. 'See you later, girls!'

'Sorry!' Alice said despairingly.

Andrea gave her a look of sympathy. 'The Keats move strikes again,' she said.

'I don't know why it happens,' Alice said glumly. 'The weird thing is that I managed to keep the doll alive today . . . I guess I have James to thank for our A grade.'

'Jay did pretty well too,' Amber said.

Andrea made a face. 'Bill and I flunked.'

'You're clearly not compatible, then,' Amber deadpanned.

They all burst into laughter.

Outside the cafe, Megan passed Thomas in the street. 'Hi, Garrity,' he said.

She scowled at him and walked on, leaving him standing in the street looking puzzled. Then he made his way into the cafe.

Inside Best Shake, the others were amazed to see

him. 'We don't see you for days,' said Andrea, 'and now you're going to say that it's a complete coincidence that you're here.'

He smiled. 'No, it's not a coincidence,' he said. 'I came along to say that you can use my uncle's warehouse in Chinatown for the rehearsals. It's completely empty right now. No one will bother you.'

Amber struck the table with her fists. 'That's fantastic!'

'But . . . how did you know we needed somewhere?' Andrea asked.

He shrugged and smiled apologetically. 'There are things I just know. That's how it is,' he said.

'But why?'

'And there are things I don't know and can't explain.' He sat down. 'Don't worry, I'll play Romeo in the show,' he told Amber.

'Great!' she said.

After a couple of minutes, he stood up to leave. 'I'm sorry I behaved so badly around you before,' he said hesitantly.

'Shall we follow him?' Alice asked the others as they watched him walk out. 'Wait!' she called after him.

'There's no point,' Amber said. 'You know he'll just disappear again.'

Andrea fought the urge to go after him. *Sooner or later, I'll find out who you are*, she vowed silently.

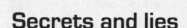

Secrets and lies

It was eight o'clock on a Sunday morning and Alice hit breakfast time singing. 'What are you doing up so early?' Daniel asked in amusement.

Her father handed her a glass of juice. 'Yeah, what is this?'

'I'm going to train with the girls,' she chirped. 'I need to practise every day to become a champion, right, Dad and Mum?'

Her parents smiled happily, but Daniel shot her a doubtful look. Her conscience prodded her again. She wasn't going anywhere near a volleyball court! She was going to rehearse her part as Juliet in *Rockspeare*.

'Why do you keep lying to them? Why can't you tell the truth?' May Rodriguez asked her as they cycled into Chinatown.

It was simple. She just couldn't bear to disappoint them.

Rehearsals for *Rockspeare* at the Chinatown warehouse had been up and running for three weeks. When

Alice and May arrived, Amber was busy checking everything, from sound and lighting to costumes. She was in her element as she moved from person to person, asking questions, giving encouragement and convincing people to stretch themselves or be more ambitious. And she was getting great results, too. The lighting was awesome and the costumes were starting to look incredible.

Andrea had unveiled the first of her painted backdrops the day before and everyone was still talking about how amazing they were.

'They're insanely good,' Amber told her.

'I don't even like painting, so it's crazy that I said I would do them, especially as you haven't helped me out with Jay,' Andrea said. 'So what's happening? I'm staying up half the night to keep my promise to you, but I'm still waiting for you to keep yours.'

Bruce, the sound guy, came up to ask Amber something about the control panel. 'Sorry,' Amber said to Andrea, suddenly distracted. 'I'll do it tomorrow. I'm just too busy with the show today.'

Andrea crossed her arms. 'You haven't changed at all, have you?' she burst out. 'You say you're doing this "for everyone", but you're just doing it for yourself! This is all an excuse to get back your queen bee status at school and on Real Life.'

'You're wrong,' Amber said, turning round and

returning her gaze steadily. 'The only thing I care about is that everyone gets the show that they deserve.'

'OK, I believe you,' Andrea relented. 'Just make sure you don't forget it.'

'Alice, May! My leading ladies,' Amber gushed, sending them straight off to try on their costumes. She clapped her hands. 'Onstage, everyone!'

Thomas ambled over to her. 'You've transformed my uncle's warehouse,' he said, looking around at all the props and activity.

She smiled. 'We're not there yet, but we're on the way,' she said breezily. Their eyes locked and her heart began pounding.

The moment was broken when Megan walked by and, turning, clouted Thomas with her guitar case slung over her shoulder. 'Ow!' he said, rubbing his head.

'Oh, sorry, Anderson, I didn't see you!' she said in an offhand tone.

'Have you finished the song?' Amber asked, wagging a finger at her. 'It was meant to be ready for today!'

'And it is ready,' Megan said brightly. 'More or less, that is. . .' Her voice trailed off. 'I just need a little more time,' she murmured. 'Please?'

'Okaaay,' Amber said. 'I guess I've got bigger

problems to worry about than your song. Like how to move all of this stuff to the school auditorium on the day, without Edward realizing what's going on. Lights, costumes, sets – it's going to be a big job.'

Alice and May called out that they were ready. 'Great, I'm coming,' she said.

Onstage, Bill Martin was dressed as a tree and he looked ridiculous.

'I'm a great actor,' he kept telling everyone. 'I'm great just being this tree. But why can't I be Mercutio?'

'Yes, why can't he?' Andrea asked Amber as she made her way to the stage. 'You still haven't cast that part.'

'Don't you start!' Amber said. 'The tree is a crucial role, Bill. Stick with it.'

'I see what you're doing there, Amber,' Bill said. '*Stick* with it, very good. But I'd prefer to *branch out*, see?'

Megan got out her guitar and started to strum. Turning to watch the commotion, she bashed Thomas again, this time on his shoulder. 'Hey, you did it on purpose this time!' he complained.

'Did I?' she said coldly. 'But why on earth would I want to hit the boy who hurt my best friend?'

The next day in the head teacher's office, Andrea and Mrs Barnes were going through the list of proposals for the annual school fundraising benefit. 'We are not selling the school bell!' Mrs Barnes was insisting, 'and I can't face another cake sale.'

'I totally agree,' Andrea said.

'What do you suggest, then?'

Andrea paused. 'How about giving extra credit to whoever proposes something that's actually workable?'

Mrs Barnes looked relieved. 'Great idea,' she said. 'I'll announce it today. Well done, Miss Tanaka!'

Andrea came out of the office feeling psyched. She loved getting praise. She couldn't wait to tell … but there was no point even trying to contact Jay. So far, he hadn't answered her calls, thirteen in total. Should she even bother trying again?

I miss you, Jay, she thought. *I don't know who to talk to when you're not around.*

Amber came out of a nearby classroom. 'Why so sad?' she asked Andrea.

'Didn't you get my message?'

Andrea opened Real Life on her phone. Her expression brightened. 'That's a great idea!' she called out when she'd finished reading. But by then, Amber had gone.

Things were getting duller by the minute at the rehearsals for Edward's minimalist version of *Romeo and Juliet*. The comments on Real Life said it all.

HELEN MASON

The first act drags on a bit!

RODNEY LEE

Isn't this the second act?

SONJA CONSTANZA

I have no idea! It's really hard to tell, especially as Juliet doesn't speak!

James was standing in for Edward while he was away. He was sitting in the front row of the theatre with a scowl on his face. Amber was next to him, sewing sacks. 'The actors could at least gesture, don't you think?' she said.

He shot her down – and when Alice asked if she could just say one line, he shot her down too. Edward's instructions to his assistant director were clear: Alice was not to say a word.

Alice felt angry and hurt. How stupid she'd been to think James cared about her! How could she have forgotten how he had treated her?

There were grumblings among the cast and crew. No one much liked Edward's ideas or directing style.

'Hey, man, it's just not working,' the sound guy said.

James's phone beeped. 'Be quiet, all of you!' he

shouted, after reading his messages. 'Edward is on his way.'

Edward arrived a few moments later, looking smug. He got up on the stage and raised his hands. The actors and crew climbed down and sat in the front rows of the auditorium.

'I have good news for you – and a surprise,' Edward said.

Amber crossed her arms. 'Is the news good for us or for you?' she asked.

His lips curled. 'Come on, don't you trust your director?'

She sighed. He never missed a chance to rub it in that he was in charge.

'As it happens, it's great news for everyone,' he went on. 'My father is bringing two Broadway theatre directors along to see our show.'

Alice yelped. 'That's amazing!' Alice and Amber locked eyes. *Rockspeare* would get a wider audience! Edward didn't realize how good this news really was.

Edward's eyes narrowed. 'And now for the surprise,' he said. 'Since we'll need a bigger audience to impress the Americans, instead of staging *Romeo and Juliet* in this miserable auditorium, we'll perform on the school football pitch!'

He didn't seem to notice that this proposal was met with complete silence.

'And in the process,' he said, his eyes blazing with the brilliance of his own ideas, 'we will make it a truly minimalist production. There will be no set, no lighting and no sound effects – just actors in sacks. It will be pure, essential theatre. It will be revolutionary!'

He looked down at his cast and crew. Frowning, astonished faces stared back at him. 'And as soon as I speak to the head teacher, it will be official,' he added.

It was clear that he wouldn't change his mind, but people tried to complain anyway. It was a terrible idea – and totally unfair of him not to consult the cast and crew. As expected, he was unmoved by their objections.

'What do you think you are doing?' Amber asked him.

'My job as a director,' he retorted. 'Just be grateful I still need you.'

'Hey, why not make it really and truly minimalist by taking away the costumes too?' she said. '*Romeo and Juliet*, uncovered?'

He smirked. Grabbing his script, he nodded to James and they left.

Amber hung her head. Had all her work on *Rockspeare* been for nothing, then? There was no way they could switch one set for another if there wasn't even a stage.

*

In the canteen, a group of boy ambushed Amber with a proposal for the annual fundraising. 'Who are you?' she asked them, as they formed a circle around her, holding their tablets, phablets and phones.

'We're the Little Big Nerds Club,' one of them explained. 'And we're hoping to get extra credit from Mrs Barnes for our fundraising proposal.'

'And what exactly is your proposal?' Amber asked.

'It's you!' he said happily. 'We propose that you give hugs to raise funds for the school.' He held up his tablet. 'We've already designed the poster.'

On the screen, there was a huge picture of Amber above the words QUEEN HUGS FOR CHARITY!

'This is a joke, right?' she said. 'I'm not hugging you lot.'

'Not just us, you have to hug the whole school!'

'Come on, everybody knows that underneath that hard outer shell you're actually really sweet.'

Amber shrank back. 'Me, sweet?' she whispered. She lowered her head and waited a couple of beats. Then she looked up again, shook her big auburn mane and roared, 'Get out of here! NOW!'

The nerds ran away as fast as their legs could take them.

What I don't need is another stupid proposal, thought Amber. *Not after Edward's rubbish idea to* move the play to the football field. If that happens, Rockspeare *is over.*

It is over, Alice thought as she punched and smashed balls in the gym. *And if* Rockspeare *doesn't go ahead, I won't be able to show my parents how important acting is to me.* She jumped up and slammed the ball over the net. *If they see me in* Romeo and Juliet, *they're really going to wonder why I told so many lies to get out of volleyball practice. Just so I could stand opposite Romeo like a stuffed dummy in the middle of the football field, saying nothing? They'll think I'm totally crazy!*

'Keats, you're the best!' one of her teammates yelled, after she spiked another ball.

My dreams are in tatters, she thought.

It was ten to three and Andrea and Bill were standing outside London's biggest science fiction megastore. Bill handed over a limited-edition issue from Jay's favourite comic series. 'You won't regret it,' he said, sucking on a milkshake.

'I'm already regretting it,' she said, shaking her head as she remembered how hard she had bargained for this comic.

It had all been Amber's idea. 'Jay's a comic freak, right?' she had written in her email. 'So show him how much you care with a comic book. I just heard on the grapevine that there's a very special sale happening this week...'

Andrea had trawled the sci-fi forums and chosen the series and issue that she knew Jay would love. The superstore holding the sale was allotting tickets online to enable people to come into the store and pick up their purchases but although Andrea was poised to click at the designated time, someone out there beat her to it.

When she found out that someone was Bill, she had some serious negotiations on her hands. First, she needed the comic. Second, she needed him to invite Jay to the store, since Jay wasn't going to come and meet Andrea of his own free will. In return, Bill wanted the moon, of course and she knew it was going to be really tricky to fix. But by time they had bashed out a deal, she was prepared to agree to almost anything.

Bill took a slurp of his takeaway shake. 'I told Jay to get here at three, sweetcakes,' he said. 'Did you talk to Amber?'

'I'll talk to her this evening, trust me. Now, get lost so I can meet Jay!' she said, anxiously looking at her watch.

He shrugged and walked away. 'One day you'll realize how much you love me, sweetcakes...'

Jay arrived a few minutes later. 'Hey, I, er, here, this

is for you!' Andrea said as he approached the shop, stepping into his path with her arm outstretched.

'Andy? What are...' He looked down at the comic. 'Huh? I don't believe it! Where did you get this?'

'Do you like it?' she asked eagerly.

'You know I do,' he said. 'But what's it—'

'A peace offering,' she said simply. 'I miss you.'

He broke into a grin. 'You got this for me?'

'Friends?' she asked.

He flung his arms around her. 'Best friends for ever!'

Ten minutes later, they were on their way to get a juice together, discussing whether they should go browsing for micro-zoology books afterwards, or just amble around counting how many floors each new skyscraper had. Andrea couldn't make up her mind. Jay was just happy to go wherever she was going.

Amber called a *Rockspeare* cast and crew crisis meeting at the Chinatown warehouse after school. Some people were reluctant to go, because what was the point, after all? If Edward was relocating the show to the football pitch, they had no chance of switching the productions around. Unlike his minimalist *Romeo and Juliet*, Amber and Megan's musical required light and sound at full blast. The costumes were awesome, the effects immense. *Rockspeare* was a big, loud, high-impact show. It was the polar opposite of minimalist and mute. It definitely wouldn't work outdoors, without a hundred imported power outlets.

Alice had to go to volleyball practice, because she knew her dad would be suspicious if she skipped it. The moment he called time, she rushed outside to unlock her bicycle, but she was hurrying so much that her fingers kept fumbling with the padlock.

That's when James came past, hands in pockets, looking downcast. 'Hi, Keats, can we talk?' he asked.

'No, we can't,' she said abruptly. She shook the padlock and cursed it for not opening.

'I'll help you,' he offered.

'I don't want your help!' she snapped. 'I don't want anything from you. Leave me alone!'

'Look, can't we—'

To his amazement, Alice stamped her foot. 'James, I have more important things to worry about than you right now,' she said.

As she marched off, he noticed that her bike padlock had finally come apart.

'You've got to let *Rockspeare* go,' May was saying. 'I don't even know why I turned up today, because it's a totally lost cause.'

'You'd give up, just like that?' Amber whirled around to face the rest of the cast and crew. 'Do you agree with this, after all the effort we've put in?'

Everyone looked glumly at the floor. It was clear that no one apart May dared to say what they were all thinking. Alice dared, but Alice wasn't thinking the same way as the rest of them.

She willed herself to say it out loud. 'I don't agree,' she murmured.

'Yeah, but you've got the most to lose,' May said.

Alice looked at her, astonished. 'We've all got a lot to lose, May! The talent and work we've put in means that this show belongs to all of us. We can't let it go. We have to fight for it! We—' She was interrupted by the doorbell.

'Are we waiting for someone?' Amber frowned. 'It could be Andrea...' She looked at the entry cam. 'Wait, it's James!'

'How can it be James?' May asked. 'Did Edward send him?'

Alice slapped a hand over her mouth. 'Oops!' she said.

'What do you mean, "oops!"?' Amber asked.

'Er, I think he might have followed me.'

'What? Go out there and make him go away!' Amber roared, channelling her inner lion for the second time that day.

'Fine!' Alice made her way down to the entrance. She needed to be strong, to be mean, to turn into an ice queen. She took a deep breath and opened the door. 'What are you doing here? How dare you? I can't stand you! Go away!'

'Actually, I just brought your bike, because it wasn't safe to leave it unlocked,' he said. 'And to say I'm sorry about the way I was earlier.'

'You always behave badly when Edward's around,' she interrupted. 'But look, I don't have time for this, I've got to get back to rehearsals.'

He frowned. 'Rehearsals for what?'

Her hand flew to her mouth again. 'Oops!'

James pushed past Alice and made his way into the main rehearsal room.

'Weren't you supposed to get rid of him?' fumed Amber, jutting out her lower lip.

James immediately understood what was going on. It didn't take a genius to realize that they were planning to put on a show to rival *Romeo and Juliet*. Despite Alice's pleas, he started messaging Edward.

JAMES COLLINS

I have something to tell you about
the show!

EDWARD BRADFORD-TAYLOR
Not now.

JAMES COLLINS
It's important, mate!

EDWARD BRADFORD-TAYLOR
I'm with my father. Tell me tomorrow.

James sighed.

'Let me guess, he doesn't have time for you?' Megan said. She was sitting cross-legged on a pile of boxes, watching intently.

'None of your business,' James said.

Amber put her hands on her hips. 'It is our business! Can't you understand why we don't want to be a part of Edward's production? He's made it all about himself. We're working hard to do something exciting and interesting – together. Surely you get that? You must be able to see that Edward is using his power in the wrong way. He's gone power crazy!'

'And his play stinks!' Megan chipped in.

James thought about Edward's bossiness and all the nasty things he had been saying about Alice – how it would be ridiculous to even think about being with drippy Disaster Keats, how awful she was in the play and how he was considering taking her part away from her. He glanced at Alice. *How wrong Edward was.*

'What do you need?' he asked simply.

'We have to change Edward's mind about staging the play on the football pitch,' said Amber. 'It's the only way we can put on *Rockspeare* at the last minute.'

'No one changes Edward's mind,' said James doubtfully. 'But,' he went on slowly, 'if he decided to do things differently . . . yes, the only way is to make him think it's a good idea to move the venue!'

'Oh yeah?' Megan said, shifting on the boxes. 'And how would you be able to—' Suddenly she lost her balance.

Thomas jumped forward and caught her in his arms.

'Careful!' he said.

'What are you doing?' Megan said irritably. 'I wasn't falling!'

'No, of course you weren't,' Thomas said with a laugh, his face close to hers. 'You were flying!'

Alice looked over and suddenly remembered the moment she had tripped over a floorboard and landed in Thomas's arms. 'Wait!' she said. 'What about the old Brick Lane Theatre? They closed it years ago, but it's still as beautiful as ever. It's a great place to stage the show. Edward won't be able to resist!'

James looked dubious. 'Why won't he? It's hardly the minimalist setting he's looking for, is it?'

Amber thought about the 'Little Big Nerds Club' and their fundraising plans. 'What about if he earns extra credit by suggesting to Mrs Barnes that the show could be the annual fundraiser?'

James's face lit up. 'Now you're talking...'

'Sounds like a plan to me,' Megan said, turning her back on Thomas.

'Over to you, James.'

The gang made their way to the theatre to check it out. 'Alice is right, it's amazing!' Amber said gleefully, once they had crawled inside.

Megan inspected a ripped seat cover. She looked up at a cluster of thick cobwebs in the corner and down at the cracked floor. 'Cleaning it up is not going to be easy, though.'

'We'll manage with everybody's help, Meg, you'll see,' said Thomas.

'My name is Megan!' she snapped. 'And we're not friends.'

Two hours later, everyone returned armed with brooms, mops, buckets and cleaning sprays. Amber gave a rousing speech from the stage. 'Here we go, *Rockspeare* team! Let's do everything we can to save the show – and that means cleaning this place from top to bottom!'

Andrea and Jay arrived to offer their help. 'Just

in time, Tanaka!' Amber declared with a wink. 'It worked, then?' she asked in a whisper as she handed Andrea a mop.

'Thanks to you and your great idea,' Andrea replied under her breath. 'But now I have another favour to ask. . .'

'Anything you want, as long as you keep on painting my backdrops. But right now, I need you to clean, clean, clean.'

A lot of effort was put in during the next couple of hours, but it was fun to be working with friends and there was no shortage of laughter. Andrea and Jay were having a mock fight with a couple of paint-splattered brushes when Thomas came up. 'One of your backdrops would look great here,' he said to Andrea, pointing at a wall panel next to the stage.

'I've done enough already,' she said, annoyed to feel her heart beating faster as she looked at him. Why did he still have such an effect on her? She flicked some yellow paint at Jay and giggled.

'Come on, you've found your love of art again, right?' Thomas said. 'Look at you: the child artist, the "little prodigy", all grown up!'

Andrea's face fell. 'Hey, that's supposed to be a secret! You said you wouldn't tell anyone.'

'What secret, Andrea?' Jay asked, dismayed to hear that she had confided in Thomas.

'Didn't you know? She's a brilliant artist and always has been,' Thomas said. He held his phone up close to Jay's face. On the screen was the original 'ideal boy' profile picture that Andrea had drawn all that time ago.

'She even drew a portrait of me!' he added.

As they recognized the picture, Jay and Andrea recoiled.

That's funny, Jay thought, *she said she'd found that picture when she showed it to me on the bus.*

How does Thomas know I drew it? Andrea wondered. *I didn't tell anyone, not even Amber or Alice!*

'What are you talking about, Thomas?' she asked sharply. *Why did he always create so much confusion in her head?*

Megan tapped her on the shoulder. 'Jay's leaving.'

Andrea whirled round and saw Jay heading for the exit. *Not again!* she thought, and ran after him.

Thomas smiled as he watched her go. He didn't see Megan swing her arm at him. He just felt a hard slap on his cheek. 'You like ruining people's lives, don't you?' she hissed. 'I really hate you, Thomas Anderson!'

As she marched off, Thomas rubbed his cheek, thinking what a strange sensation the slap had triggered. Momentary pain, yes, but also something else.

I'm doing what I have to ... so why do I have a knot in my stomach? he wondered. *What does it mean?*

Andrea followed Jay into a park opposite the theatre. When she caught up with him, he was standing in front of a small fountain with his hands dug deep in his pockets.

'Jay?' she said, her hand hovering behind his shoulder – almost touching him, not quite daring. 'I'm sorry I didn't tell you about my drawings, but you need to understand ... it was really complicated. You see, I suddenly stopped when I was a kid ... and then I started again recently, but it was a secret thing and I just felt I couldn't share it...'

'But you shared it with Thomas,' he stated.

She sat on the ground. 'I made a mistake,' she said. A cool breeze rustled the leaves in the trees all around them.

'OK.' He knelt next to her.

'OK?' she repeated.

'I'm not really mad at you, Andy.'

'No? Because I would understand if you were – and I'm mad at myself for making such a mess of things, because—'

'Andy, I like you,' he interrupted.

She smiled. It was such a relief to hear him say those words. 'I like you too – you're my best friend in the world,' she said, 'the best friend anyone could have, the best—'

He stood up. 'You don't understand! I like you! In that way.'

She stared at him, astonished.

'Since the day I met you, I've thought you were the most incredible, intelligent, special girl. . .'

She went on staring at him.

'And also the most beautiful,' he added, only half believing that he'd managed to say the words he had rehearsed in his head for so long.

Andrea couldn't look at him any more. *Oh no!* she thought. *What do I say? How do I tell him – it's not like that for me?* She shivered in the chilly night air. The silence was unbearable. Jay's shoulders were drooping under the weight of it.

Say something! Andrea told herself.

'Hmm, it's really cold out here, isn't it?' she said.

'Yeah, it really is,' he agreed awkwardly. He was looking into the distance too. 'In fact, it's freezing. See you inside.' He walked away.

Her head dropped into her hands and she sat in stunned silence for a few moments. *Brilliant,* she thought. *The first boy who tells me he loves me and I break his heart. Life is so unfair!*

Hidden feelings

By the next morning, *Rockspeare* was back on. James had spoken to Edward, who had discussed it with his father and approached the head teacher. Of course, Mrs Barnes was delighted by his brilliant idea to combine the end-of-year show with the annual fundraiser.

In the computer room, Alice jumped for joy. 'We did it!' she said. 'Thanks to you, James.'

'There's still a lot to do,' Amber warned, 'but we've won this battle, at least.'

Amber went off to find Andrea, leaving James and Alice feeling awkward on their own. There was a weird anticipation in the air, with too many words flying around unsaid. She broke the silence first. 'I have a class soon,' she said.

'Me, too, must go,' he mumbled. He suggested meeting in the canteen hall later. 'Only because I don't feel like eating alone, of course,' he added.

'Oh,' she said, thinking how graceless he could be. *Who are you, James?* she wondered as they walked along the hallway. *Sometimes I think you're my Prince Charming, other times I really can't stand you.*

'Anyway, thanks for helping us with *Rockspeare*,' she said. 'It can't have been easy to go against your best friend.'

He made a face. 'He deserves it and I deserve a better friend than him.'

She couldn't think of anything to say, then. The silence was excruciating. Finally, something occurred to her. 'Oh, what was it you wanted to tell me yesterday when I was trying to unlock my bike?'

He turned and gazed into her eyes. Her heart started thumping. 'This,' he said, kissing her gently on the cheek.

It was Alice's first kiss, with the boy she'd had a crush on for ever – and it was out-of-this-world-dreamy-wonderful-flowers-floating-everywhere.

Andrea had messaged Amber to meet her in the school courtyard. 'Hi, what's up?' Amber asked when she saw her.

Andrea was smiling in a strangely fixed way. 'Hiya,' she said. 'Remember that favour I asked you about?'

'More or less,' Amber said suspiciously. She didn't have time for anything that wasn't related to *Rockspeare*.

'Well, he's here,' Andrea announced in a sing-song voice.

Bill stepped forward – dressed in a suit, wearing a tie and carrying a bunch of flowers. He looked really odd. 'Babycakes, your prince has arrived!' he gushed at Amber.

'Oh no,' she said. 'Andrea?'

But Andrea was already making her escape. 'I'll paint you another backdrop for this,' she promised.

'Bill, I don't want to go out with you,' Amber said. *Wait*, she thought. *Has he shaved off his disgusting goatee?* She peered closer. No, he had just neatened it up. She noticed that his suit pockets were bulging. With biscuits, no doubt. Ugh.

'I don't want to, either,' he said. 'But I do want to be Mercutio in *Rockspeare*!' He went down on one knee. 'Let me try out for the part, please? I'm not going to let this one go, director.'

Andrea Tanaka, you'll pay for this!

Andrea tried to make it up with Jay by giving him a rare vintage action figure. But he wouldn't accept it – and even she had to admit that an action doll was no substitute for a girlfriend. What was she thinking? She couldn't blame him for walking away as he had, shaking his head in disbelief. First, she had broken his heart, then she had tried to paper over the cracks in their friendship with a man doll. She had messed up – big time.

The challenge now was to make things better. She decided to approach the problem like a maths equation. What result did she want? She wanted Jay to be happy. How could he be happy? If someone mended his heart. Who could mend his heart? Not Andrea, unless she suddenly started liking him in that way. So... That was it! Jay needed a girlfriend! OK, that was the theory side of the problem solved. Now for the hard part – the practical side. How was Jay going to get a girlfriend? A dating site? No, he'd hate that. A blind date? Maybe, but she still couldn't see him agreeing to it. How about if she set him up with someone without him knowing?

Yeah, right – and how was she going to do that? How would she find the right girl, for a start? Jay was special. He needed to be with someone equally special. She started looking through the profiles of the students on Real Life. It would be perfect if she could find him someone at London International High School, but what were the chances? *Close to zero*, she thought, as she zipped through one profile after the next.

Likes: fashion and shoes.
Likes: pit bulls and kickboxing.
Likes: embroidery and kittens.

No. No. No.

Wait a second! What about this one?

Time to play cupid!

Amber passed Lynn in the hallway and did a double take. Hey, snap! Pink top, mauve scarf, shark's tooth necklace, jeans and brown leather bag.

Amber's ex-friend was walking around in exactly the same clothes as she was!

Amber scowled, bit her tongue and walked on. *Don't say anything*, she told herself. *It doesn't matter. Lynn's just a sad copycat, a queen without her own style.* She pulled off her scarf and tied it around her waist, instantly transforming her look. She felt better already, but ... the necklace had to go. She couldn't believe that Lynn had bought exactly the same one.

Opening her locker to see if she could find something to wear in its place, she pulled out a crown pendant with a gold chain. It was a necklace that Edward had given her, months ago, when they'd been in love – and when they'd split up, she had told him that she would never wear it again. But ... did it really matter? More to the point, did she care? She decided that, if she liked the necklace, she should wear it.

Amber made her way to meet Megan, who was helping to organize the set move from the Chinatown warehouse to the Brick Lane Theatre. Dylan was using the Sad Cats band van to carry all the equipment from one place to the other. By the time Amber caught up with Megan he had already made one trip.

Alice had messaged to say that her granny wasn't well and she wouldn't be able to help. Amber had told her not to worry.

Dylan's van drew up. 'Do you need to check in with James?' Megan said.

'Good point,' Amber said.

AMBER LEE THOMPSON
Can you confirm our plans? Is he with you?

JAMES COLLINS
Double affirmative. Don't forget, the name's
Bond...

'Hi, girls!' Dylan said, opening up the side of the van. Megan grinned.

Inside the van was Dylan's friend Alex. 'Get in, doll,' he said with a wink, when he saw Amber.

She rolled her eyes and climbed inside the dusty van. *The things I have to do for this show!*

Right on cue, just as fencing practice was ending, James posted that he was in a relationship with Alice Keats.

DANIEL KEATS
?????

But only one comment was of any interest to James.

EDWARD BRADFORD-TAYLOR
Loser

James flew across the gym floor. 'Delete that comment!'

'Why should I?' Edward sneered. 'It's true, Keats is a loser and, therefore, so is anyone who wants to be with her.'

James put up his blade. 'Delete the comment now!'

Edward put up his sword. 'If I win, you dump Keats and change your status back.'

James put on his mask and smiled behind the mesh. Edward had taken the bait. Now he just had to keep him fencing until he got the all-clear from Amber.

At the theatre, Thomas turned up just as the others were lugging the final load inside. 'Can I help?' he asked.

'No, we don't need you,' Megan snapped. She made a mental memo to ask Amber if it was OK to hate Thomas as well as Edward. She wasn't sure why, but she really, really disliked him.

'Actually, I think we do need him,' said Alex, struggling under the weight of a background panel. 'Mate, can you help me with this?'

They found hiding places for almost everything. The stage trapdoor proved useful and they stashed away the scenery panels backstage. But there was nowhere to put the audio equipment, which had to go in the middle of the room, according to Amber.

'I know a place. Come with me,' Thomas said.

'OK, but let me check everything is under control at the other end,' Amber said.

She messaged James, but he didn't reply.

In the gym, James and Edward were behaving like two of the Musketeers, parrying and thrusting their blades while they exchanged bitter insults. It was a wonder they weren't putting on French accents too.

'Surrender!' Edward cried as he pounced forward. 'Admit you're no match for me and say goodbye to that beanpole!'

James parried. 'You haven't won yet! And don't talk about Alice like that – or you'll regret it!'

Edward snorted behind his mask. 'Don't tell me you like that wet rag. For goodness' sake, get a grip!'

James knocked the sword out of his hand. 'I told you to stop it!' he yelled – just as Mr Bradford came through the door with Mrs Barnes by his side.

'Eddie!' he boomed.

'Dad?' Edward took off his mask. 'What are you doing here?'

'Hello, Mr B,' James said.

'Your father is here to collect you,' Mrs Barnes said. 'You are excused from lessons for the rest of the afternoon – as are you, James.'

'B-but why?' Edward asked, hoping his father hadn't seen James knocking his blade out of his hand.

'Because as usual you haven't thought things through, son,' his dad said, barely disguising his irritation.

'Why, what's going on?' Edward asked.

His father glared at him. 'That theatre you picked is a dangerous wreck. It's a massive problem, but I'll fix it, like I always do. Come on, we're going there now to assess the damage.'

James began to panic. *To the theatre? I must warn Amber!*

'Wait, let me get my phone,' he said to Edward.

'Forget it, you're not going to need it,' Edward said, pushing him forward. 'I'm sure the beanpole will survive without hearing from you for the next hour.' As they stepped out of the building, it started to rain. 'This might come in handy, though,' he chuckled, passing him a big red umbrella.

Before school finished, Andrea broke into Jay's locker and stole his bike padlock keys. She padlocked his bike to Sara Parker's and returned the keys to his locker before the last bell went.

As LIHS students flocked out of their final lessons of the day, she hid behind a tree and waited to see what would happen. Soon Jay was standing by his bike, scratching his head in confusion. 'I locked my bike to someone else's?'

He looked around and saw a girl sitting on a bench reading a comic. She was wearing glasses like his and a beanie hat over her long wavy brown hair. 'Is this bike yours?' he asked.

She smiled. 'Yes.'

'Why aren't you standing here, fuming about the idiot who blocked your bike?'

'Because I thought the "idiot" would probably come along soon, and in the meantime it was an excuse to read my favourite comic for the twelfth time.'

She didn't need to say another thing – Jay was smitten. He recognized the edition she was reading, even though it had been reprinted with a new cover. They talked about the artwork and he asked if she'd like to go to the comic megastore with him.

'Sure,' she said. 'But have you been to the new King of Comics on the other side of town? I could take you there.'

'Why not?' he said.

Andrea watched them cycle away together. *They look happy*, she thought. Her plan was obviously working. *So how come I'm not smiling too?*

Mr Bradford's car sped through the rain towards the Brick Lane Theatre. From behind the wheel, he was giving Edward and James a lecture about not doing their research properly. 'As usual, I have to pick up the pieces,' he said angrily. 'If it weren't for me, you would have worked on the show, only to find that the theatre wasn't fit for use. So now we have an appointment with the owner to survey the old place and agree on a price.'

Mr Bradford's phone rang.

'The investors have arrived. What should I do?' his PA asked on loudspeaker.

'Ask them to wait, while I sort out yet another one of my idiot son's predicaments. I'll be there when I can.'

James felt sorry for Edward, despite everything. His dad was so mean to him. He wondered how to help his friend. 'Mr Bradford, you're the best,' he said. 'When the show goes on at the theatre, the whole school will be jealous of Edward's success, especially as he's such a talented director.'

Edward gave him a surprised smile. But Mr Bradford didn't appear to be listening.

James sat back in his seat and started worrying how he could warn the others that Edward was about to arrive. As the car drew up outside the theatre, he had a brainwave. He grabbed the umbrella that Edward had brought and pretended to grapple with it, in preparation for getting out of the car. In the process, he managed to slide forward and press the car horn with the umbrella tip.

'What are you doing?' Mr Bradford yelled.

'Sorry, it opened automatically!' James said, using the umbrella to beep the horn a few more times – 'accidentally'.

'Enough! Close the umbrella, you clumsy fool!'

'I'm trying!' James said, hoping that Amber and the others had heard.

The owner of the theatre met Mr Bradford, Edward and James at the car.

'Everything all right?' he asked.

'Yes, thank you, just having a moment,' Mr Bradford blustered, getting out and straightening his suit jacket.

'Sorry, my fault,' James said, suddenly understanding how Alice must feel when she had one of her #embarrassingmoments. There was nothing more he could do to delay Edward and his father. All he could do was keep his fingers crossed that Amber and the others had been warned. He entered the building, scanning the auditorium for signs of their presence, unaware that they were hiding in a cupboard, scared stiff, listening for voices. As the owner told Mr Bradford how happy he was to be selling the theatre to someone who planned to renovate it, he and Edward drew up next to their hiding place.

'This is exactly what my play needs, right, James?' Edward was saying.

James thought he heard a scuffling sound. 'Huh?' he said, finding it hard to concentrate.

Edward sat down. 'The contrast between the ornate splendour of this place and my minimalist production will make it even more spectacular,' he went on.

Inside the cupboard, Amber held her breath. They were too close for comfort! She reached to fiddle with her necklace, but it was gone. 'Oh no!' she whispered. 'If Edward sees it lying around, it will give us away!'

Thomas put a finger to his lips to shush her and crawled out of the cupboard on his hands and knees. James spotted him and immediately manoeuvred Edward away, trying to keep a straight face.

'It's a great venue,' he agreed. 'But we're not done yet, Edward. I beat you at fencing. Now you have to delete that comment about Alice on Real Life.'

Edward frowned. 'Will you stop it? I didn't lose!'

James opened his eyes wide. 'Come on, I disarmed you. That's losing,' he said. 'The Edward I know isn't the type to go back on his word.'

A couple of feet away from them, Thomas reached forward to where Amber's necklace was lying on the floor and picked it up.

Gritting his teeth, Edward took out his phone and deleted the comment, just as Thomas crept back into the cupboard.

'Come on, let's go,' called out Edward's father. 'I have more important business to get on with.'

'We're coming!' Edward said. He turned back to James. 'Don't think I don't understand what's going on. You can't trick me,' he said.

What's he talking about? James thought guiltily. *Does he suspect something?*

*

Andrea felt strangely tired as she walked home from school. She was pleased to read Amber's relieved messages.

AMBER LEE THOMPSON
Mission accomplished! We did it!

But she didn't feel like responding.

A notification from Jay came up on her phone. He was with Sara Parker at King of Comics.

Glad they're still together, she thought. Then she remembered the time she had been to the store with Jay. It had been fun. They'd laughed a lot.

An hour later, Real Life announced that Jay was at Funland with Sara. *How funny – she'd taken Jay to Funland for the first time*. It was a place she always associated with him.

Next they were at the London Eye. With a pang of jealousy, Andrea realized that Jay was taking Sara to all of 'their' places! But she called herself up on it instantly. *How selfish was she? This wasn't a question of territory. As long as they fell in love, it didn't matter how or where.*

But when Jay posted that he and Sara were at Endless Books, she fought the urge to throw her phone out of the window. Endless Books was her special place. *That's enough!* she thought, disabling the notifications.

But her phone kept beeping. Jay and Sara at the National Portrait Gallery. She tried to turn it off, but half an hour later it beeped again. Jay and Sara at Canada House.

'Turn off! Turn off!' she yelled at it.

She sat down to study. But she couldn't concentrate and the notifications went on coming through. She kept thinking about Jay and the times he had helped her, all the fun they'd had together, their in-jokes and made-up words.

Oh, no. Surely she wasn't . . . she couldn't have got it so wrong . . . she didn't. . .

No, of course not!

Outside the theatre, Megan and Dylan were having an argument. He was refusing to give her a lift home with the heavy amp she was carrying. 'But my house is on the other side of the city!' she said. 'I'll have to drag it.'

'What's going on?' Thomas asked Amber.

'He's been nice to her all day. I knew it wouldn't last – he had to break at some point,' she whispered.

'Stop complaining!' Dylan shouted. 'All you do is stress me out. "Help me move my friend's scenery!" "Lend me the sound mixer for the show!" "Help me compose the final song!"' He slammed the side door of his van. 'Do something on your own, for once.' He got in the van next to Alex. 'I'll call you,' he said, without looking at her.

Megan had a lost look in her eyes as the van drove away. 'Ignore him, I'll help you,' Amber said. 'Will you give us a hand, Thomas?'

'We don't need him,' Megan said.

'Let me carry the amp,' Thomas said. 'Or at least we can take it in turns.'

'Thank you,' Amber said.

He smiled at her and she felt as if he'd just pumped her heart up with helium.

The double-decker bus to Brixton went past.

'My bus!' Megan yelled.

They had to run, but they made it – just about. Thomas grabbed Amber's hand and pulled her along for the last fifty feet. His touch made her shiver. As they got on the bus, she realized that she had left her bus pass in Dylan's van. 'Leave it to me,' Thomas said, using a spare Oyster card to pay her fare.

'A queen should never pay,' he added.

She was astonished. *He was Prince Charming again?*

'Actually, I'm not queen of anything any more,' she grumped, making her way up the stairs behind him.

He turned and gazed into her eyes. 'To me, you'll always be the queen.'

She couldn't understand it. He hadn't even wanted to kiss her – but now he was playing her knight in shining armour again? It was definitely time to confront him.

'You know what?' she said, jabbing her finger in his face. 'When you talk like that, I don't know whether to kiss you or hit you.' She paused, for effect.

'But since you don't want my kisses, I guess I'll hit you!' she declared, bashing him playfully on the shoulder.

The woman in the seat in front of them turned round and told them off.

'You're in a public place!' she reminded them. 'Behave.'

Amber sat down. 'Sorry,' she said, trying hard not to giggle. 'You're completely right.'

They had to fight down their laughter for the next twenty minutes, until the woman finally got off the bus.

'Where are you going?' Edward asked James when they got back to school.

'To get my phone,' James said sharply.

'What's wrong, mate? We've always been so close. Why have you been so serious lately? Is it that clumsy blonde's fault?'

'Don't call her that!' James said.

'I know all about it,' Edward went on thoughtfully.

James started. Was he referring to *Rockspeare*?

'You suggested the switch of venue so that she would get to act in her dream theatre, didn't you? You can't fool me. You're clearly under her spell. Whatever happens, I won't give her any lines back,' Edward said with his usual sneer. 'What do you see in her, anyway?'

'What did you see in Amber?' James asked him.

Edward's face fell. 'Come on, there's no comparison. . .'

'Isn't there?' James said, walking away, out of the school gates. 'Think about it, mate. Only one of us is single. . .'

Actually, he needed to check that statement. Alice had agreed to bait Edward with a relationship status notification, but did she want him to delete it now? Or did she want to be his girlfriend? When he got home, he messaged her, but couldn't bring himself to ask directly.

JAMES COLLINS
About that relationship status . . . it's still
up, you know.

ALICE KEATS
Oh, and if we leave it?

JAMES COLLINS
It means we're really together. So. . .?

ALICE KEATS
Are we or aren't we?

JAMES COLLINS
Hey, I asked first!

*

'Is it hard to write a song?' Thomas asked Megan as the bus rumbled on. He seemed genuinely interested.

'It depends,' she said. She didn't really want to discuss it – especially not with him.

'The *Rockspeare* song is obviously very difficult,' Amber joked.

Megan made a face. 'I'll write it tonight, I promise!'

'I don't believe you,' Amber said. It wasn't a challenge. She seemed to have lost faith.

'It's not my fault if *Romeo and Juliet* is a boring play,' Megan said.

'You're so wrong. It's actually beautiful,' Thomas said. 'Romeo and Juliet shouldn't love each other. Destiny is against them, so are their parents. No one wants them to fall in love, but they can't help it! They're not supposed to, but they do it anyway. I think it's a really special story.'

Amber looked at the floor and thought about what he'd said. Everything was telling her not to fall in love with Thomas, and yet she couldn't help it –

but they weren't like Romeo and Juliet ... because he didn't love her back. Did he?

The bus trundled over London Bridge, heading towards Elephant and Castle and onward to Brixton.

'Hey, what's that?' Thomas asked, pointing at the river.

'What do you mean?'

'That,' he said.

'Are you talking about the Thames?'

He looked transfixed, full of wonder, like a kid seeing snow for the first time. 'I guess so, I've never seen it before.'

'You live in London and you've never seen the Thames?' Megan said. 'You're a strange one.'

If only you knew how strange, Amber thought. But she wasn't telling.

She was forgetting that sometimes good friends don't need to be told. Megan could sense something, anyway.

'Everything's OK,' Andrea was telling herself, even though she knew it wasn't.

Setting Jay up had seemed like the perfect solution to his heartbreak problem. But seeing him with someone else had changed everything. Her theory-and-practice equation was void – because she hadn't factored in her own feelings! She, Andrea, was the biggest idiot in the universe. Because, after all that had happened, she finally realized she liked Jay.

In that way.

*

When they arrived at Megan's house, the girls hugged and said goodbye. Megan grudgingly thanked Thomas for helping out, but wouldn't take his hand when he offered it to her.

Amber and Thomas walked away.

'Can I ask you something?' Amber said.

'You want your necklace back?' he asked, reaching into his pocket.

That's it! she thought. She stopped walking and looked him straight in the eye. 'Will you do something for me?' she said.

'Er. . .'

'Will you vanish now, like you always do? Please?' she said. She turned away, broke into a run and disappeared around the next corner.

'Wait!' he called after her.

But Amber didn't intend to wait for Thomas any more. She had waited for him long enough. On her way home, alone, she sent him a message telling him to stay away from her.

Megan's mum, Rachel, tried not to show her alarm when she heard that her daughter had been hanging out with Thomas Anderson and she respected Megan's wishes not to be disturbed while she sat up all night writing her song for *Rockspeare*.

In the morning, Megan messaged Thomas.

MEGAN GARRITY

I wrote the track! It's about Romeo and the sea –
the first time he sees it, he thinks about Juliet.

THOMAS ANDERSON

Can I hear it?

Afterwards, she wondered why she had played it to him, rather than to Dylan or Amber. She wondered why it had made her so happy when he said it was a beautiful song, and that he was sure Amber would love it. After all, who was Thomas Anderson? Wasn't he someone she hated?

She lay back on her bed, thinking about his deep, dark eyes. At least she knew one thing for sure – she would never fall for the boy her best friend loved. That could never happen, however gorgeous he was. She woke up two hours later in a cold sweat.

'Oh no,' she whispered to herself. 'Megan, no!'

Star-crossed lovers

Alice's mother couldn't help laughing as she put away the washing. What was she doing humming nursery rhymes to herself? Her kids were all grown up now. Daniel was a talented young man heading for a career in professional football and Alice was a promising volleyball player. At that very moment, they were both at practice, honing their skills, taking their responsibilities seriously. She smiled with pride. Her babies were so busy that they might not even make it home for supper!

She heard a beep as she passed the computer in the dining room. *Strange*, she thought. *I didn't think it was switched on*. She took a look at the screen. *Even stranger. Alice's profile page, on Real Life, open for all to see?*

Emily Keats put her head on one side. A notification had just appeared.

'Final rehearsal for *Rockspeare*: NOW! Go, Alice, you're the world's best actress!'

*

At the Brick Lane Theatre, James found Thomas messing around with his phone backstage. 'Come on, Romeo!' he said. 'You're the only one missing!'

Amber was standing on the stage giving one of her rousing speeches.

'Now that Romeo has finally joined us, I just want to say thank you,' she said. 'You've all helped to make *Rockspeare* the most amazing show our school will ever have seen – and you've done it through your unbelievable hard work and incredible talents. When we go onstage on the 16th, we'll show Edward and Mrs Barnes they were wrong! And we'll give the audience the best show of their lives!'

The rehearsal got underway and everything went super-smoothly – until Thomas started climbing a tree to kiss Alice on her balcony. Since it wasn't any old tree – it was Bill Martin, and Bill didn't much like being climbed, there was a slight commotion when Thomas used Bill's head as a step on his way up for the big kiss.

'Noooo, stop!' Amber yelled, suddenly panicked by the idea of Thomas kissing Alice, even if they were only acting.

'It wasn't good?' Alice asked, her heart sinking. It was a key scene and she had rehearsed it over and over. If it wasn't right by now, she was unlikely to nail it in time for the big day.

'You were amazing, Alice – and so was Thomas,' Amber said, quick to reassure her leading actors. 'No, the problem is Bill,' she added.

James nodded. 'The tree really isn't working.'

'Oh, isn't it?' Bill said angrily. 'I'll show you.' He ripped open his tree costume to reveal one of the outfits that Amber had made – for Mercutio.

'What are you doing? Stop it now!' Amber exclaimed. 'Do you know how long it took me to make that tree costume?'

'By my heel, I care not,' he replied in a loud, clear voice. 'Good king of cats, nothing but one of your nine lives; that I mean to make bold withal, and, as you shall use me hereafter, drybeat the rest of the eight.' He stumbled and clutched at his chest. 'Ah, but I am hurt! I am sped!'

Falling to the floor, he murmured, 'It's a scratch, a scratch . . . marry, 'tis enough. . .'

There was silence in the auditorium as he acted out Mercutio's death. Then he leapt to his feet again, as Bill. 'So, after that heartfelt display of pure talent, do I still have to be the tree, or can I play Mercutio?'

Everyone looked at Amber. She paused, keeping a straight face, and then broke into a grin. 'The part is yours, Bill!' she declared. 'You're amazing.'

He gaped at her. 'I did it?' A huge cheer went up and everyone started clapping. 'Yay!' he yelled, clapping along with them. 'I knew it! I'm the greatest actor in the universe!'

The rest of the rehearsal was a breeze.

ROCKSPEARE GROUP

AMBER LEE THOMPSON

Well done, everyone! You were perfect today.

Bill couldn't resist making a play for Andrea as the sets were coming down. 'Soon I'll be a famous actor,' he boasted proudly. 'So take advantage of my offer now – or join the queue later. . .'

She pretended to consider it. 'Thanks, anyway – but I'll take a risk on the queue option,' she decided.

She knelt down and started folding a cloth backdrop. *If only she hadn't said no to Jay*, she thought. She was really missing him now. Like, really, really missing him, off the scale.

'Andrea?' said a voice.

She looked up. 'Jay!' she said happily. 'What are you doing here?'

Her smile froze when a girl stepped forward and took her place beside him.

'My friend Sara wanted to see the theatre – and I thought it would be great if you met each other,' he said, as if it were the most natural thing in the world to be introducing her to his girlfriend.

'So, you're Andrea,' Sara said warmly. 'Jay's always talking about you.'

Andrea wasn't the giggling type, but right then she giggled. 'Hi Sara, great to meet you,' she said, determined to keep her smile going even though her face had started to ache.

The moment Amber saw Megan, she jumped on her about the song. 'Is it ready? I need it yesterday!'

'Just give me two more days,' Megan pleaded. 'It's nearly there, but I've got the Sad Cats concert tomorrow night. I can't finish it until after that.'

Amber gave her a worried look. 'You know I can't do without that song, Meg!'

'I know. You'll get it, I promise.'

Thomas caught Megan's eye – she returned his gaze so defiantly that he decided told not to ask her why she had lied about the song to Amber. Instead he wandered off to an empty part of the theatre and messaged her about it on Real Life.

THOMAS ANDERSON
Why did you say that? You played me the song.
It's finished.

MEGAN GARRITY
I don't like it any more. It's too mushy.

THOMAS ANDERSON
What's wrong? Are you angry about something?

MEGAN GARRITY
None of your business. Now stop writing to me.

How strange, he thought. That unfamiliar sensation was back that only seemed to be triggered when Megan got angry with him. What did it mean? How was he supposed to react?

He noticed Amber watching him. She quickly looked away. He turned and walked towards her. 'About what you wrote the other day. . .' he started.

'If you have something to say, please say it quickly, or shut up,' she said. She had managed to keep it together since her outburst over the kiss, but now she was really hurting inside. She couldn't stop thinking about Thomas but he didn't need to know that. She didn't want to risk opening up to him again.

She started to move away. 'Wait!' he called after her. 'There are things you don't know about me. . .'

She turned around to face him. 'So, tell me.'

He hung his head. 'It's so strange . . . I don't even understand them myself.'

'Come on,' she said irritably. 'I've had enough of your excuses.'

'They're not excuses,' he said, moving closer to her.

'I want . . . I need . . . to talk to you, about us. Just give me a chance to explain. Please?'

'When?' she demanded.

'Tomorrow night, at the Sad Cats concert?'

She stuck out her lower lip. 'OK,' she said. 'But only if you promise not to vanish again. Agreed?'

He smiled. 'OK.'

When she had gone, he tried to enter the concert as a date in his Real Life diary. But the social network blocked him. He tried again. His phone was telling him that the only available event to him was football practice.

'Come on!' he said, feeling totally confused. 'Why are you doing this? What's happening?'

Walking their bikes home after the rehearsal, James and Alice found themselves having another of their awkward, going-nowhere conversations. She asked about the football finals. He asked about the volleyball finals. Between each answer, there was a sticky pause.

She sighed inwardly. *What's going on with you, James? Why aren't you telling me you like me?* She messaged Amber and Andrea for help.

AMBER LEE THOMPSON

What's the problem? I thought you two were together.

ALICE KEATS

Now nothing's happening.

AMBER LEE THOMPSON

If you want to be with him, you have to tell him.
Boys are hopeless. Take it from me!

ALICE KEATS

But what do I say?

AMBER LEE THOMPSON

Anything! Just don't talk about the weather.

The weather? Alice thought. 'Nice evening, isn't it?'
she said.

'If you say so,' James replied moodily.

ALICE KEATS

Whoops, I mentioned the weather!

ANDREA TANAKA

Alice, don't throw this chance
away. Declare your love, before
it's too late. . .

Andrea knew all about it. In her case, she had left
it so late that she had set up the boy she liked with

another girl – and now she was messaging Alice from a smoothie bar, where she was sitting opposite Jay and the girl she had set him up with.

Sara was calling him 'Jay-Jay' and smiling stupidly at him. Worse, Jay was looking totally gorgeous, even when he was smiling stupidly back at Sara.

Why hadn't she realized how fantastic he was?

He turned his attention to Andrea. 'So how's it going? Did you enrol to apply to the summer courses at Yale?'

'Yup,' she said, feeling slightly happier. At least he was still thinking about her.

'That's brilliant!' He turned to Sara and explained that Andrea was a total genius. Sara smiled and looked interested, but something in her expression hinted that she'd heard it all before.

'I have to put in a super-long essay with my application,' Andrea said. 'But you'll help me, won't you?'

Jay didn't hesitate. 'I'd really like to, but I'm afraid I can't.'

Andrea was stunned.

'The thing is,' he went on, 'I want to go to America too, to learn how to draw comics.' He grinned. 'Sara told me about this course in New York—'

'Everyone knows about it,' Sara cut in.

'Did I tell you Sara loves comics too?' Jay said. He

turned to Sara. 'Andrea wouldn't know about the course,' he explained. 'She's a genius, but not when it comes to the comic world.' He turned back to Andrea. 'So anyway, my parents say I can go if I get good grades at the end of the year!'

'That's fantastic,' Andrea said, sensing his excitement.

His face lit up. 'Yes, and Sara's aunt and uncle live in New York and they've said they'd help us find a place to live.'

Andrea's heart sank. So he was going to be spending all summer with Sara?

'I really want to be an illustrator,' Jay went on. 'So keep your fingers crossed for me, won't you?'

Andrea raised both hands, fingers crossed. 'Of course!' she said, putting on her brightest smile. She looked at her watch and stood up. 'Whoops, got to go and study. Let's catch up tomorrow and you can tell me all the details!' She waved furiously as she dashed off. 'Great to see you, Sara,' she called.

She felt devastated on her way home. Clearly, there was no way she would be able to study. *I've lost him*, she thought, *and the only person I've got to blame is myself.*

She stopped and looked up at the night sky. I just wish I'd realized how much I liked him.

*

Alice and James were cycling side by side along the road. 'I'm going this way now,' she said, pointing left.

He pointed right. 'I'm going that way.'

She didn't know what to say. 'OK, see you tomorrow?'

I don't believe this! she thought. *He's going to let me go, just like that?*

He screeched to a halt. 'Wait a minute, you! Where do you think you're going?'

She jumped off her bike and into his arms. 'You and I are together, silly,' he said, hugging her close.

Relief flooded through her. 'Why didn't you say so before?'

He cupped her face in his hands and looked deep into her eyes. 'Are you joking? You didn't seem to want me to, that's why.'

'But it's all I wanted!' she said.

He laughed softly. 'How am I supposed to know if you don't tell me?'

She laughed with him. 'We've been so stupid!' she said, hugging him again.

He took her hands and clasped them in his. 'Keats, there's something I've been wanting to ask you … what about Thomas?'

She felt herself stiffen. *Thomas*, she thought, losing herself in a dream of the past. *The boy who encouraged me to act, who helped me to find my confidence and stand*

227

up for myself. My very own Romeo, who seemed to like me – but didn't want to kiss me.

Can I forget him? she wondered. *I want to, because I really like James now. But how can I explain the muddle of feelings inside me? Can I make James understand? Or should I just lie, and say Thomas means nothing?*

'James, I—' She was about to go on when her phone rang. 'Wait, it's my mum,' she said, answering the call. 'Yes, Mum. What? When? I'm coming right now!'

'What is it?' James asked worriedly.

Alice quickly got on her bike. 'Sorry, I have to go,' she said, cycling away.

'Wait!' he called after her. 'You didn't answer my question.'

Alice got home to find Daniel with a plaster cast on his foot. He was limping around with the aid of crutches. 'What happened?' she asked.

'Sprained ankle,' he said. 'Rotten luck, huh?'

She rushed over to hug him. 'Did you do it playing football?'

He shook his head. 'That's the stupid thing! I was moving the gym lockers with Thomas and Ross, I lost my footing and one of the lockers fell on my leg. Thomas called the nurse right away—'

'—and I called your mum!' said the school nurse, coming out of the kitchen carrying a first-aid bag.

That's impossible, Alice thought. *Thomas was with us at the theatre.*

'What are you doing standing up?' Emily Keats chided Daniel. 'Sit down at once!'

'Sorry, Mum,' he said.

'And you three mustn't tire him out,' she warned, looking sharply at the others.

Alice sat next to Daniel on the sofa. 'Will you be better in time to play in the football final?' she asked.

'No way,' he said miserably. 'The team will have to do without its captain.'

'Well, at least you'll be able to uphold the Keats family reputation at the volleyball final, right, Alice?' the nurse said.

Alice felt a prickle on her neck. 'Who, me? Yes, of course. And we'll definitely win.'

He mother gave her an odd look. 'Hmm, but what about *Rockspeare*?' she asked.

Alice sat up straight. 'Oh.'

'Yes, your father and I have discovered your little secret,' her mother went on, 'and, forgetting the fact that you're probably going to be grounded until Christmas, we'd like to know what's going on.'

The truth was out. They knew that she'd been going to rehearsals. They knew about the old Brick Lane Theatre. And they knew that she'd been getting her volleyball teammates to cover for her.

What she couldn't stand was how sad they seemed. They were such lovely people, such amazing parents. Their disappointment was unbearable. 'You lied to us every single day,' her mother said. 'Are you going to lie to us again?'

'I'm sorry,' she said at last. 'I'm really, really sorry. I shouldn't have lied. It was completely wrong. But you need to know that it's over now, because I've realized that acting isn't important to me. It took a while, but now I know for sure that volleyball is my priority. It's all I want to do – really, it is. So I've quit *Rockspeare* to focus on my training. Honestly, Mum, Dad – you have to believe me!'

They stared hard at her, their sadness showing in their eyes. But she had convinced them. They believed her.

Did it mean she was a good actress? She didn't care. She hated lying.

But what was the alternative?

At school the next morning, everyone was talking about Daniel on Real Life.

JAMES COLLINS
Is that why you ran off, Keats? I'm so sorry.

JESS BAGLEY

Daniel? Are you OK? Can I come round to see you?

DANIEL KEATS

Sure, Jess. It's only a sprained ankle.

JESS BAGLEY

I'm on my way! ♥

AMBER LEE THOMPSON

Get better soon, Keats!

Amber couldn't stop thinking about her hot date with Thomas that evening.

'You've got a date with Thomas Anderson?' Megan said in disbelief, when they met up in the courtyard during break. 'And you're coming to the concert together?'

'Thanks, that's just the reaction I was looking for.'

'But you can't trust him! He's treated you so badly!' Megan protested. 'Are you really going back for more of the same?'

Amber smiled dreamily. 'This time it's different, I promise.'

'Oh yeah? That's what Dylan tells me every week!'

Amber's expression turned serious. 'Thomas isn't

the one who's different, I am,' she explained. 'I really like him. Hey, do you remember that game we used to play? Close your eyes and you'll see the boy you love?'

'Yes, and we never saw anyone!'

Amber chose to ignore this observation. 'Well, every time I close my eyes, I see his face – and I'm sure he's feeling it too. It can't just be me.'

Megan smiled at her best friend. 'Oh, good luck, then,' she said, hugging her. 'I hope it goes really well. I'm sure it will – because I'll have my fingers crossed all night!'

'Thanks, Meg,' Amber said gratefully. 'See you tonight.'

'Sure – I'll be the one playing the guitar with crossed fingers.' Megan laughed. As she walked away, she closed her eyes and opened them again.

'Stupid game!' she muttered to herself, shaking her head to get the image of Thomas out of her mind.

Alice sat by the side of the volleyball court with her head in her hands. Her father was nagging a couple of the other players about their timing.

'Everyone on the court!' he said finally. 'Let's do a little volleying.'

Alice barely heard him. One thought kept circling her head. *How do I get out of this?*

Coach Keats walked over to his daughter. 'Darling,'

he said in a low voice, so that none of her teammates could hear, 'are you sure you were telling the truth last night?'

She stood up, smiling broadly. 'Of course I was!' she said, and she ran onto the court.

Now that Daniel was out of the football final, she knew that all her parents' hopes hung on her. She felt watched, scrutinized, out of control.

She automatically volleyed the next ball that came her way. *It feels as if I'm not even here*, she thought.

Andrea knew what she had to do. First, she cancelled all her study appointments on Real Life. Then she asked for an extension on her science assignment. It was the first time in her entire school career that she had asked for extra time.

'Tanaka turn an assignment in late?' she overheard someone say as she strode purposefully down the corridor. 'Clearly, the world is ending.'

She went straight home and started preparing her art materials.

It was her father who spotted her carrying several large canvases into her bedroom. 'Is she doing what I think she's doing?' he asked her mother.

Joelle Tanaka grinned. 'If she is, I've been waiting for this moment for years,' she said.

Sitting in her bedroom, in front of the first blank

canvas, Andrea narrowed her eyes. It wasn't going to be easy, she realized. She wasn't just painting *Rockspeare* backdrops now. She was creating a visual narrative that would change with every scene, connecting images that only Jay would understand. And it was going to take a lot of work.

This is the only way I can tell him what I don't have the courage to say, she thought.

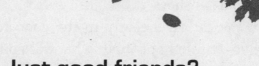

Just good friends?

Amber sent Megan a photo of her date outfit – a dark red mini dress with a silver belt.

AMBER LEE THOMPSON
How do I look? Will he like me?

MEGAN GARRITY
If he doesn't like you, he doesn't
deserve you! You look great!

Amber's mother was waiting downstairs to give her a lift to the venue.

'Are you ready to rock out at the Sad Cats concert?' she asked her daughter.

'Hmm, we clearly come from different centuries, Mum, but yes, I'm ready to go,' she said bounding down the stairs two at a time.

'Darling?' her mother said. 'Aren't you forgetting something?'

Amber looked down at her feet. She had forgotten

to put on her shoes?

In the car on the way to the concert, her mum tried to draw her out about what was going on in her life. Was she still with Edward? How were Lynn and Jess? What kind of show was she designing for?

'I don't want to talk about it,' she said in a bored voice, looking absently out of the car window.

'OK, whatever you want,' her mum said. 'But if you're forgetting to put your shoes on, would I be right in thinking there's a boy involved? Someone new, perhaps? Someone special?'

Amber laughed. Her mum got that right. 'OK, if you must know, I am meeting a boy,' she said. 'Oh, Mum, he's so gorgeous. I know it sounds silly, but I swear he's perfect. There's no one else like him. He's just. . .' Her voice trailed off as she thought about Thomas.

'You've got it bad, huh?' her mum said under her breath. 'Good luck, baby.'

Backstage at the concert, Megan was shouting at her phone. So far, Thomas Anderson had tried calling her six times – and it was driving her crazy. 'Stop it!' she yelled. 'Go away!'

Dylan told her to take a chill pill. 'We're going onstage in two minutes.'

'I'm perfectly calm,' she snapped back. 'You're the one who's making me nervous. Where's my red guitar pick? You know it's my favourite.'

He shrugged. 'Dunno.'

'As usual, you couldn't care less about the things that matter to me. You're an idiot, Dylan!' She stormed off.

And I'm even more of an idiot than you are, she thought.

A few minutes later, Dylan introduced the band onstage. The crowd went wild. Among them was Amber, wondering where Thomas was. Edward was there, too, searching the sea of blue- and purple-lit faces for Amber. Eventually he saw her and made his way over, with James following behind. 'You look beautiful,' he said.

She scowled at him. 'Leave me alone! I'm not here for you.'

'Maybe it's better to let her go, mate,' James said, putting a hand on his friend's shoulder.

Edward turned to face him. 'That's great advice from someone who doesn't even know where his clumsy blonde girlfriend is!' he said vengefully. 'Have you checked she's not with Anderson?'

While the music blared and the lights danced over the crowd in crazy patterns, James went off into a corner and messaged Alice again.

JAMES COLLINS
What happened to you? I'm at the concert.

You're here too, right?

But Alice was at home, lying across an armchair, staring at the ceiling. *No, I'm not there, James,* she thought.

She composed a message and sent it out to the *Rockspeare* group.

ALICE KEATS
I don't know how to tell you all this, so I'm just going to say it. I don't want to be your Juliet any more, so I'm quitting *Rockspeare* and I'm quitting Edward's play too. I'm sorry. Really sorry.

James saw the message first. Then Amber, followed by Andrea. James told Edward that Alice was quitting.

'What's going on, James?' Edward yelled over the noise of the band.

But James didn't know. He wondered why she hadn't said anything.

'You don't know?' Edward shouted. 'You're meant to be her boyfriend!'

'And you're the director! Perhaps you should have thought more carefully about taking all her lines away.'

Edward scanned the crowd again. He saw Amber sitting down with her head in her hands. As he approached, she got up to leave. 'Wait, don't go!' he said. 'Amber, I'm sorry. Please forgive me.' He hung his head.

Edward apologizing? she thought. *This I have to see.* She stood and waited, hands on hips.

'Losing you was the biggest mistake of my life,' he said, his top lip trembling slightly. 'I've been an idiot and I apologize for everything I've done.'

Not bad, she thought, sitting down next to him. 'Thanks for saying it, but it's too late. You know that, right?' she said.

'But you can still be Juliet,' he said eagerly. 'This is a sign, don't you see? Alice has quit, but you'll be a better Juliet – the best Juliet – and you'll have the costumes, the lines, whatever you need, I promise. Everything can go back to the way it was before.'

She raised her eyebrows. 'The way it was before? The Amber you're imagining doesn't exist any more, Edward – and you know it.' She stood up and turned away. 'I've forgotten about you. It's time you did the same.'

'Never,' he declared.

'Too bad.' She gave her hair a flick and strutted off.

But her cool composure masked the fact that she was worried she still hadn't seen Thomas. OK, it kind of paled into insignificance next to Alice's bombshell, but she was still curious. The date had been his idea. *Where was he?*

She was wondering what to do next when Andrea rushed up, looking flustered. 'Nice outfit!' Amber said, taking in her paint-splattered hoodie and jeans. 'I can see you really made an effort.'

'Yeah, funny,' Andrea said. 'But there's no time for hilarious jokes. We can't let Alice do this – to herself or to us! It's her parents' fault – they must have found out about *Rockspeare* and made her quit acting.'

'But what can we do?'

'Go and see her! Be her friends. Support her, help her – and talk to her parents, if necessary.'

Amber gave her an amused look. 'Are we really that good friends?'

Andrea jabbed her with a finger. 'Do you have a better reason to stay here?' she asked. 'Something more important than *Rockspeare*?'

'I guess not,' Amber said regretfully. She messaged Thomas on their way out.

AMBER LEE THOMPSON
Please don't leave – wait for me. I'll be
back soon.

The gig ended and the crowd roared their approval. Onstage, Megan and Dylan made a big show of high-fiving each other. 'You were great, baby,' he whispered.

'Leave me alone,' she hissed back.

Thomas was waiting for her backstage. 'Hi Meg,' he said. 'I'm looking for Amber, have you seen her?'

She walked right past him. 'No.'

He caught up with her. 'You were great onstage. . . I mean, the Sad Cats are really good.'

'Yeah?'

He put his hand out to shake hers. 'Truce?'

'Why? We weren't fighting,' she grumped.

He gave her a pleading look. 'Why are you so angry with me, Meg?' he asked.

'Why do you care?' she said. 'You have Amber . . . and I have Dylan.'

Something snapped in Thomas. 'You've been annoyed with me ever since I met you and why? For what? I have to tell you, Garrity, you're getting on my nerves. You're unpleasant and irritating! You behave as if you're perfect, as if you never do anything wrong . . . and the worst of it is that I can't ignore you,' he went on. 'You're doing my head in – but I can't get you out of my mind! You confuse me. You make me doubt the things I'm supposed to do. You make me doubt myself. . .'

Neither of them had noticed that he was slowly moving closer to her.

'. . .and I don't know what. . .' He leaned forward and wrapped his arms around her. It felt magical.

Suddenly she was running, as far away from him as she could get.

'Megan!' he called, distraught.

But she didn't hear him. She refused to hear him. *This is the boy my best friend is in love with*, she thought. Her mind was in turmoil. *I can't fall in love with him too, I can't. . . I can't.*

Alice's parents almost didn't let them in. 'I'm afraid Alice is grounded,' her mother said.

Amber and Andrea assured them that it wasn't anything to do with *Rockspeare*. Lie, lie, lie. It was something really important about, er, Bill Martin – could they go in? Please?

'You have five minutes,' said Coach Keats.

Alice seemed shocked to see them when she opened her bedroom door.

'What are you two doing here?'

'We've come to rescue you!' Amber said, immediately going over to check out the contents of her wardrobe.

Andrea put an arm around her shoulders. 'I'm sure we can persuade your parents to change their minds.'

'That's what friends are for!' Amber added.

Alice shook Andrea off. 'Friends? That's a joke!' she said.

Amber whirled round to face her. 'What do you mean? We helped you, supported you and put you in the show! Don't let us down now because you're scared to tell your parents the truth.'

Alice pointed at her bedroom door. 'Go away!'

'Why? We're your friends,' Andrea said. 'Really, we are.'

'You're not! You're only here for selfish reasons – because you don't want me to quit *Rockspeare*. Real friends try to understand each other. They tell each other what they're feeling, don't they? So why haven't you, Andrea, told us that you're in love with Jay? It's so obvious from the way you look at him that you're jealous of Sara, but do you share it with us? No, you don't. And why haven't you, Amber, admitted that you still like Thomas?'

Neither Andrea nor Amber could think of an answer. 'But I . . . er, you see. . .'

Alice spoke for them. 'Why haven't you talked about it? Because we're not friends, we never have been and we never will be! Now, go!'

They left in silence.

*

Alice sat on her bedroom floor wondering if she'd done the right thing. Yes, she decided. Amber and Andrea weren't her real friends. They'd proved that with Thomas and *Rockspeare*. In their world, it was every girl for herself.

And yet they'd changed everything for her – they'd changed her life, really. Or was it Thomas who'd done that? It was confusing.

She was in the right – she was sure of it – but did it really matter now that she was on her own?

'So you still like Thomas?' Andrea asked Amber as they walked down the street towards the underground.

'It's none of your business,' Amber said.

'True.'

As they went separate ways, Andrea started asking herself questions. She wondered if she'd really been such a bad friend. Actually, she didn't think so but Alice had been adamant.

Oh, who cares? she thought resentfully. *I won't be seeing her or Amber now that Rockspeare isn't happening.*

And without *Rockspeare*, she wouldn't be able to tell Jay how she felt about him, either. Since she no longer had any friends to advise her, that was surely the end of it. It was all over. She was on her own now.

*

I don't care! Amber thought. *Disaster Keats means nothing to me. Arrogant Andrea can go and take a jump too. I can do fine without them both –* and Rockspeare.

But it was funny being alone. It wasn't a familiar feeling . . . or a particularly nice one.

She looked around the empty concert venue. Thomas was nowhere to be seen – he hadn't waited for her, as she'd asked him to. She picked up her phone.

AMBER LEE THOMPSON

Thomas, where did you go? What happened?

He didn't reply.

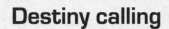

Destiny calling

A thin stream of sunlight shone through the curtains of Amber's bedroom and onto her sleeping face, like a mini-spotlight.

'Get up, sweetie!' her mother called, knocking on her door. 'It's your big day!'

Amber stirred and rolled over. 'I'm not going,' she mumbled. 'Leave me alone.'

Her mother obviously didn't hear her, because she didn't respond. Amber grabbed her phone. Still no word from Thomas.

Nothing was going on in the Real Life *Rockspeare* group, either. She pressed delete. It was time to move on.

A notification appeared.

WARNING
Are you sure you want to delete this group?

Of course.
Goodbye to everything I wanted to do, she thought. *Goodbye to all my new friends.*

What next? Her phone rang.

'Bill, there's no way I'm playing Juliet again!' she said. 'Not for *Rockspeare*, not for Edward's play!'

'Romeo, wherefore art thou?' Bill replied in a high-pitched voice.

'And no, you can't play her, either. You're good, Bill, but not that good!' She hung up.

Everything's gone wrong, she thought. She looked at her phone again.

It was weird – even though she and Thomas had never been together, she missed him so much that it hurt. She felt lost without him. What was keeping them apart? She sent him a message.

AMBER LEE THOMPSON

I have no idea where you are, but I'm
thinking about you.

The moment she sent it she wished she hadn't. Amber Lee Thompson, chasing a boy? It was unthinkable. And yet, now that Andrea and Alice were no longer her friends, what else did she have? *Who* else did she have? Apart from Thomas.

She fell back on the bed. *I'm not leaving my bedroom until I hear from him*, she decided.

*

Andrea's mother couldn't understand it. 'Shouldn't you be at the theatre?' she asked. 'The show starts in a couple of hours and you're the set designer.'

'Leave me alone, Mum,' Andrea said, opening the front door. 'I'm not interested in being a set designer. I'm a student and I need to focus on my grades, so I'll be staying late at school today – and tomorrow, and the next day.'

Once she'd left, her mother turned to her father and shrugged. Together they went up to Andrea's bedroom and looked through her work. 'All these beautiful pieces... I thought being the show set designer was reminding her of how much she loved painting.'

'You never know,' said Mr Tanaka. 'She might still change her mind.' He held up a painting that he'd found under a pile of half-finished canvases.

'Does this remind you of someone?'

'It's Jay,' Joelle said. 'How strange. What else don't we know about our daughter?'

As she walked through the school gates, Andrea realized that she needed to go back to her old ways, her old self. *No more friends or perfect boys, no more stupid plays*, she thought. *Just me and my books, that's all I need.*

She had assignments to catch up on, an essay to write for the Yale application ... she would be too busy to feel lonely. Anyway, books were great companions, as she had learned at an early age, as a typical only child, reading for hours in her bedroom.

'Hi Andrea!' She saw Jay and Sara along the hallway, waving and smiling at her.

'Hey!' she called out, in the warmest, sincerest tone of voice she could summon. Then she made a quick turn into the nearest classroom, willing it to be empty.

It was a maths classroom – and it wasn't empty. In fact, it was packed out with students. Standing in front of the blackboard, the maths teacher greeted her like a long-lost friend. 'Andrea Tanaka, the star of the school! Come and help me explain definite integrals to my sixth-form class.'

'Me?' she said, glancing at the long equation he had written on the board. She couldn't remember a single thing about definite integrals. The numbers and symbols made no sense to her.

'Come on, don't be shy,' he said, beckoning her. 'I know it's a little advanced for your year, but you're way ahead in this subject.'

She moved towards him like a zombie. 'Here you go,' he said, dropping a piece of chalk into her hand. 'Now, show us how it's done.'

*

Alice was sitting on the team bus, wondering if she would ever feel happy again. Her acting dreams were over. She'd fallen out with her friends. All that was left was volleyball.

A chant went up at the back of the bus. 'Go, go, go, London International Volleyball Team!' her teammates were shouting. 'Go, Alice, super-spiker!' someone yelled.

At least she was pleasing her teammates – and her parents. She was glad about that. They deserved it.

But will I be happy? she wondered.

On the pavement outside Megan's house in Brixton, the Sad Cats were getting ready to go to rehearsal. Dylan was talking about the new song he wanted to try out when Megan took his hand. 'We need to talk,' she said.

'Now?' he whined. 'Let's play first and chat later, OK?'

'No, we're talking now,' she insisted. She yanked him away and into the house.

'What's going on with you?' he demanded. 'You've been acting really stupid recently.'

She looked at the floor. How did you tell the boy you'd always loved that you weren't sure if you loved him any more? Memories of their time together swirled in her mind. The laughter, the moment they decided to start a band, their first gig . . . it had been two brilliant years and they had shared so many fantastic experiences.

'Dylan, I need time apart from you.' *There. She'd said it.*

'What?' he said, looking at her with a stunned expression. 'Are you dumping me?'

She clenched her fists. 'I didn't say that. I just need time to figure things out, because I'm not sure any more. . .'

'That's the stupidest thing I've ever heard. Either you want to be with me or you don't.'

She sighed. 'That's what I'm saying, I need some time to think.'

'Forget it, I'm tired of you and your doubts. And you know what? You can have all the time you want, because I'm breaking up with you.' He headed for the door.

'Wait,' she said. 'Don't go. Let's talk.'

'Dylan Simmons doesn't wait for anyone,' he said, stomping off. 'And you can forget about the Sad Cats too! The band just officially broke up.'

She stood on the doorstep and watched him leave.

It's all my fault, she thought. *But how can I help feeling the way I do?*

Things had been going wrong between her and Dylan for a while, and Thomas had brought that into focus. It started to rain, which suited her mood. Like the sky, she felt like crying because although she didn't love Dylan any more, she knew how much she was going to miss him.

Just then, her mother came home. 'What's happened, darling?' she asked. 'Don't stand out in the rain getting soaked! Come inside.'

She led Megan inside and put the kettle on. 'What were you thinking?' Rachel asked. 'You'll make yourself ill!'

'Oh, Mum!'

The doorbell rang and Megan ran to answer it. 'Dylan, you—' she started saying as she opened the door.

But it wasn't Dylan standing on her doorstep in the pouring rain, with his hands in his pockets, looking sad and bedraggled – it was Thomas.

'Hi, Garrity,' he said. 'Can I talk to you?'

Her head started spinning. 'Yes?' she said, wondering what was coming next.

'What happened at the concert – between you and me – can't happen again,' he said haltingly, his eyes glittering with tears. 'I . . . it was beautiful. But I have to think about Amber. I have to think about Alice and Andrea, too. They're my destiny, not you.' He lowered his head. 'I'm sorry.'

He turned and left.

Megan felt like her heart was suffocating. She ran back into the house and threw her arms around her mother. 'Mum, help me! I feel horrible,' she sobbed.

That was Thomas Anderson! Rachel thought. *What's he doing here?*

'Don't worry, darling, it'll be OK,' she said to Megan, stroking her hair.

'Oh, my little girl, nothing can hurt you now.'

It's happening again, she thought. *I don't know how or why, but Thomas Anderson is Adam Burton – and, like Adam, he's here to ruin everything.*

She flashed back to a memory of the time she had to calm and soothe her friend Lisa, just as she was calming and soothing Megan now.

I won't stand by and watch this time, she vowed. *I can't let what happened to Lisa so many years ago happen to my Megan too!*

Amber's mother burst into her room. 'That's enough, young lady!' she said. 'It's time to get up and face the world.'

'Get out of my room,' Amber moaned, from where she had retreated under her bedcovers.

'Not a chance,' her mother said. 'I've even selected what you're going to wear today.'

Amber sat up. 'You have?' Her mother held up one

of her new designs – it had long sleeves, a full skirt and funky embroidery on the shoulders and hem. She loved it. 'It's beautiful, it really is,' she said. 'I'm still not going, though.'

But her mother was having none of it. 'It's your responsibility to be backstage,' she said, shaking her head at all her daughter's objections and excuses. 'You say you're only the costume designer. You should know better than that! Look at this dress, for instance – it's only a heap of shapes sewn together, isn't it? And what holds all the pieces together?' she asked.

'Er, I don't know, Mum,' Amber said. She had no idea where this was going.

'You do know!' her mother said. 'What holds it all together is the thread. Without the thread, it's not a dress; it's just a pile of rags. And you know which kind of thread is best? The kind that can't be seen...'

Amber smirked. 'Are you saying I'm a piece of invisible thread, Mum?'

'Why not?' her mother said with a giggle. 'You're not playing Juliet, are you? But you are holding the production together. So you'd better get going – because it will all fall apart without you, believe me.'

Amber leapt out of bed. 'You're right, Mum. I love you,' she said, giving her mother a hug.

If I give up, it's over, she thought. *I'm the one holding everything together.*

She started plotting while putting on her make-up. She needed to get *Rockspeare* up and running again, which meant pulling Alice back into the production. First, she reopened the Real Life *Rockspeare* group and sent a message.

Andrea saw the notification come up while she was in the library. *But what if I just want to go on studying?* Then she remembered. *Wait, the backgrounds for Jay!* She got up from her seat and sprinted out of the room.

Next, Amber wrote to Alice.

AMBER LEE THOMPSON

I know you hate me and you think I'm not a real friend, so maybe you don't want to read this. But right now it really doesn't matter if I'm your friend or not. I just want to say that I've seen you acting. I know how great you are. Don't make the biggest mistake of your life by skipping the show. Your destiny isn't to play in the volleyball final – it's to go onstage. It's the only way you'll be happy.

On the team bus, Alice had moved to a seat at the back. When her father came over, she was staring vacantly into space. 'This is yours,' he said, handing her phone to her.

'Thanks, I must have left it up front.'

'By the way, I couldn't help seeing that your friend Amber has sent you a message,' he added. 'And I think she probably has a point.'

Alice looked down at the screen.

AMBER LEE THOMPSON
Run. We're waiting for you.

She scrolled down and read the rest of the messages.

'Dad?' she said, looking up at him in disbelief. 'Are you saying that it's OK if I don't play in the final?'

He beamed at her. 'That's exactly what I'm saying,' he said. 'Because it's not what you really want, is it? Volleyball's not your thing. You want to act – and I need to give you the chance to follow your dream.'

She could barely take it in. It was that easy?

'Really?' she said. 'But you and Mum—'

'Your mother and I just want you to be happy,' he said firmly, 'and you didn't seem very happy for a while back there. We thought that volleyball was the answer, because playing a team game can do wonders for your confidence and sense of achievement. We thought we were doing the right thing, especially as you were a naturally talented player. We didn't know you preferred acting. . .'

'. . .because I didn't tell you,' she said.

'If you'd talked to us, we would never have tried to push you down the wrong path,' he went on. 'We're here to help you, kiddo. We want the best for you.'

'So ... what do I do now?' she said, her heart thumping.

'You follow your dreams,' her dad said. He put his face against the bus window and scanned the street. 'There it is!' he said under his breath. He whistled to the bus driver and asked him to stop.

'What are you doing?' Alice asked.

He was already getting off the bus. 'Wait,' he said. 'I can't turn the bus back but I can help you get to the show on time.'

She looked out of the window and saw ... a bike shop?

Her dad was already on his way inside. A couple of minutes later, he appeared with a bicycle – complete with shopping basket and child seat.

Alice jumped off the bus. 'You bought me a bike?'

'It's a bit beaten up, but the guy in the shop says it flies like a rocket.' He produced a helmet and helped her adjust the straps. 'Go to the theatre, now. Make me proud,' he said.

'I will, I promise,' she whispered, her eyes welling up with tears. She jumped on the bike and cycled off at full pelt, using every ounce of energy she had to pump the pedals.

'Hurry!' her dad called after her.

'I'm hurrying,' she yelled back, even though she was out of earshot. 'For you and for Mum, the best parents in the world.'

Backstage at the Brick Lane Theatre, everyone had the jitters. Everyone except Amber, it seemed. For the past hour, she had been constantly saying the same thing, over and over again. 'Just don't worry! Alice will be here. Try to stay calm and leave the details to me.'

As the tension levels rose, she wondered just how long she could go on repeating herself. She didn't have to wait long for an answer. One of the sound guys came up to her, white as a sheet, looking like he was about to be sick, and started jabbering about the sound box.

'Stop it!' Amber said firmly. 'Pull yourselves together right now, everybody! It's going to be fine!' That seemed to do the trick.

Amber had to have faith, but she knew she was on shaky ground. Andrea hadn't turned up with the backdrops. That was a big problem. And although she was convinced that Alice would be on her way, would their leading actress make it in time for curtain up? The audience was beginning to file in. They didn't have long now.

Just then, she saw Andrea, walking towards her,

head down, carrying a bunch of rolled up canvases. 'Hey!' she said, unable to disguise her relief.

Andrea looked her straight in the eyes. 'I'm here for the show, not for you,' she said frostily.

Amber's friendly smile disappeared as she switched to professional mode.

'Fine. Are those the backdrops?'

'That's right,' Andrea said. 'But you can't look at them yet.'

'Well, I'll just have to trust you, then, won't I? OK, wait for my signal and then switch them with Edward's backdrops. Tim and Rodney will give you a hand.' She turned and walked away.

Andrea felt guilty. *Why am I being like this? We're supposed to be friends and I'm treating her like a stranger.*

She sighed. It was her own fault. She wanted to admit to Amber how terrified she was about revealing her feelings for Jay, but didn't know how to find the words. She looked over at Amber, who was talking to Bruce about uploading the *Rockspeare* playlist. Next she was reassuring some of the actors that Alice would be arriving soon. 'Listen up, everyone,' she announced. 'Edward is about to arrive, so I'm going to stay quiet from now on. I'm the costume designer, remember? Nothing more.'

'Right, boss!'

*

Out in the auditorium, Edward was keeping his father company while they waited for Mrs Barnes to arrive. James was hovering behind them, with one eye on his phone as he waited for news from Alice. Mr Bradford's face broke into a wide grin. 'The Pfeiffers are here already,' he said. 'Come with me, son.'

Edward looked a picture of ease and charm as he shook hands with Elizabeth and John Pfeiffer, 'the best theatre producers in the world', according to his father. But inside he was quaking.

'Now go and do yourself proud,' his father said, dismissing him. He sat down with his friends and started cracking jokes.

'Those were the Broadway producers,' Edward told James, as they made their way backstage.

'I can't believe they actually came!' James said.

Edward frowned. James had never seen him look so worked up. 'What's the news from Alice?'

'She's not answering,' James said.

'Call her again!' Edward commanded. He saw Amber ahead of him. 'Do you think she'll come?' he asked her.

Amber laughed. 'Does it matter? You can always replace her with a cardboard cut-out.'

'Cardboard can't act,' he snapped. 'I need an actress!'

Amber knew he was appealing to her to take

Alice's place, but she wouldn't and couldn't agree to that. Still, she felt sorry for him. She could sense how wound up and tense he was and it was all because of his father and his deep fear of disappointing him.

She took his hand and gave it a squeeze. 'Everything will be OK,' she said.

'Just in time, mate!' Bill called over when he saw Thomas arrive backstage. 'If you'd left it any longer, I would have had to take your place as Romeo!'

Amber marched over to Thomas. 'I'm really angry with you!' she said, jabbing the air with her finger. 'Where were you?'

He looked at the floor. 'I'm sorry, Amber, I—'

She saw Edward coming towards them. 'We'll talk about it later. It's time to get ready now.' She reached up on tiptoe to whisper in his ear. 'For *Rockspeare!*'

Megan arrived, looking downcast. 'Is the song ready?' Amber asked her.

'Yes, and it's great!' Megan said, brightening up. 'I know you're going to love it.'

Edward walked by. 'Garrity! What are you doing here?'

'Calm down,' she said coolly. 'I just came to wish my friends luck and now I'm out of here.'

The tension in the air was increasing with

every second. There was some clapping from the audience, a few shouts. 'Come on! Why are we waiting?'

A runner came with a message from Edward's dad. 'He says he'll leave if it doesn't start soon. He's got better things to do than hang around, he says.'

Edward's hands were clenched and his lips white with anxiety when Alice finally burst into the backstage area. 'I'm here!' she said, panting.

James stepped forward. 'You made it!'

'Yes, and I have so many things to tell you,' she said breathlessly.

Edward yanked her by the arm towards the dressing room. 'You've kept us waiting long enough, Keats. Get ready now!'

In the dressing room, Amber helped Alice put on her flowing Juliet costume for *Rockspeare* and then tucked it up inside the sack she fitted over the top of it.

'Thanks for sending the message. I wouldn't be here if you hadn't,' Alice said gratefully.

'No problem, Keats — but we'll talk about it later, OK?' Amber said. 'Just make sure you take off that horrible sack the moment you get onstage.'

This is it, Alice thought, taking a quick look at herself in the mirror. *I really am Juliet! I'm about to go onstage and make my dream come true.*

We've finally made it, Amber was thinking. *The show that we've all helped to create is about to become real.*

Andrea was behind the stage curtain, peeking out at the audience. *There's Jay! He has no idea I'm about to tell him how I really feel about him.*

At last Edward went onstage. A smattering of polite applause greeted him.

'Ladies and gentlemen,' he said, after it had died away, 'it is with great pleasure that I would like to introduce the London International High School end-of-year show.'

'Go, Ed!' someone shouted.

Edward laughed. 'Thank you! But before the curtain goes up, I have an announcement to make. I've played a trick on everyone – and now is the time to come clean. For months I've led you all to believe that we've been working on a stripped-down production of *Romeo and Juliet*, with minimalist costumes and a mute Juliet. In fact, the truth could not be more different. And so, ladies and gentlemen, please put your hands together for the most spectacular version of *Romeo and Juliet* you will ever see. It's entitled *Rockspeare* – and I hope you enjoy it.'

There was a big burst of applause as he left the stage, and a sense of excitement filled the auditorium.

The noise floated backstage to where Amber, Alice and the rest of the cast and crew were standing in shocked silence.

'How did he find out?' Alice whispered.

Everyone looked at Amber. 'I don't know!' she said, throwing her arms up.

'What do we do?' people started asking.

Alice was still trying to work it out. 'Someone must have told him,' she said.

'You got that right, super-brain,' said a voice behind her. Alice whirled round. Lynn was standing at the door, looking ultra-sleek and very pleased with herself. 'Surprise!' she said with a self-satisfied smile.

'Lynn? What's it got to do with you?'

'Have you forgotten that my best friend just happens to be going out with your brother?' Lynn said. 'After Daniel sprained his ankle, he told Jess that your mum had been asking you about *Rockspeare*. Not *Romeo and Juliet*, see? Something else altogether. Well, he was curious, and Jess told me and I . . . well, I have my own way of finding things out. Of course, I had to tell Edward.' She shot a look at Amber. 'We're very close, you know.'

Amber scowled.

'You ruined everything!' Alice said, her voice cracking.

Lynn's dark eyes glittered. 'You're the one who started it, Disaster Keats!'

Just then, Daniel walked in, using a stick to support his ankle. Alice turned to him, distraught. 'Can you believe that Jess told Lynn about *Rockspeare*?' she asked him.

'I told her to!' he blazed. 'You deserved it, Alice. What you did was wrong. You tricked Mum and Dad. You tricked me and you tricked Edward. You didn't play fair.'

She looked at him in utter disbelief. 'But you're my brother!'

'I don't care. You lied to me,' he said, shaking his head.

Amber stepped forward to say something, but Edward cut in. 'So what are you going to do?' he asked her. He stood in front of her smiling broadly, his hands dug into his pockets. She fought the urge to leap at him, screaming.

'You could still pull the show,' he said. 'But then everyone in the class would get a fail... Or we could go ahead...'

'And you would get all the credit,' she said scornfully.

He chuckled. 'You can't win, can you?'

The cast and crew gathered round them. May Rodriguez was the first to speak. 'I won't go onstage if you don't want me to, Amber,' she said.

'Me, neither,' said Bill.

Soon the entire *Rockspeare* company had agreed that they wanted to stand by their director. They were prepared to fail the class and sacrifice their grade for Amber.

'Thank you, everyone,' she said, tears pricking her eyes. 'I appreciate your loyalty.'

What do I do? she thought, as they waited expectantly for her to speak.

She made her decision in seconds. Much as she hated the idea of Edward taking the credit for *Rockspeare*, she wasn't going to wreck Alice's dream of acting in front of her parents, or May's and Bill's ambitions, or Andrea's new-found love of painting, or the many talents that had come together to make *Rockspeare* the great show it was. She wasn't going to waste all the work the crew had put in, either.

She thought about the conversation she'd had with her mum earlier. OK, no one in the audience would know that *Rockspeare* was an Amber Lee Thompson production. They wouldn't know that she had produced and directed it, that she had joined all the different pieces to make a whole. But she would still be the invisible thread holding it all together – and because of that her friends and fellow students would get to perform and show off their incredible skills and artistry. *Rockspeare* had always been a team effort. It didn't matter who got the credit for it – she just had to do the right thing.

'We're going onstage,' she said, clapping her hands. 'Everybody take your places.'

Show time!

For the first fifteen minutes of the show, Amber was too busy organizing the cast and crew backstage to take in what was happening out front. But after that there was no doubt in her mind that *Rockspeare* was a hit. It totally rocked. It was obvious that the audience was loving it because applause kept breaking out in the auditorium. Everyone behind the scenes was happy and excited.

Alice ran on and off stage, her eyes bright, her cheeks flushed – every inch the besotted teenager with poetry in her heart and everything against her. She really was Juliet – she and everyone else had forgotten that Disaster Keats ever existed. As for Thomas, he was every girl's dream of Romeo – bold, gorgeous and daring – and it was easy to see how Juliet would want to risk everything for him. May was awesome as the nurse and, to the audience's surprise, Bill was a very charismatic Mercutio. Thanks to Amber's styling, he was also charming and good-looking.

Juliet's outfit teamed biker boots with a brocade

fitted coat and floaty dress. Romeo wore a loose woven shirt, a sword belt, jeans and trainers. Mercutio postured and gestured in a top hat. Amber's vision for *Rockspeare* was perfect and everyone agreed she had nailed it.

She giggled as she read the latest post on Real Life.

RODNEY LEE

To all the people who aren't at the Brick Lane Theatre now, you're losers!

Coach Keats was watching a live feed on his phone, tears rolling down his cheeks. He barely noticed when the school volleyball team romped to victory. 'Keats is a strange man,' remarked the coach of the opposing team. 'He doesn't even bat an eyelid when his team wins the inter-school finals!'

The team gathered round him, jumping around and screaming. 'Coach, we won! We're the champions!' they kept yelling.

Still he didn't look up from his phone. 'I'm so happy,' he kept saying. 'So happy.'

Amber went looking for Andrea and found her outside the set room, dragging a box of rolled up backdrops towards the exit. 'Where do you think you're going?' she asked.

'I've changed my mind,' Andrea said. 'I can't put my paintings out there after all.'

Amber folded her arms across her chest. 'Don't you think it's a bit too late to back out now, Tanaka?'

'They're my paintings and I'll do what I want with them!' Andrea said, glaring at her.

Amber didn't bother to reply. She called over a couple of the stagehands and told them to put the paintings in position ready for the final scene.

'You can't do that!' Andrea hissed.

Amber grabbed her hand and clasped it tightly. 'It's for your own good, Andrea, trust me.'

Sitting next to Sara in the stalls, Jay watched the final scene unfold in shock. As each of Andrea's backdrops was highlighted in turn, he recognized scene after scene from their friendship – of the two of them studying in the park, drinking shakes in a juice bar, wandering downtown, browsing bookshops... At the very moment Romeo was saying to Juliet, 'Look at the stars. They're full of our memories,' Jay was confronted with some incredible memories of his own.

He felt confused. *Romeo and Juliet*... Jay and Andrea? Did that mean...? Right then, a message from Andrea came through on his phone.

ANDREA TANAKA

You've probably guessed already. I like you too!

JAY WILLIAMS

You're an idiot, Andrea.

ANDREA TANAKA

I know!

Juliet awoke to find Romeo dead and Shakespeare's tragedy began to take its final deadly course. Just then the air was filled with the haunting sound of Megan's voice. She was singing the song she had written for Thomas, with her guitar as sole accompaniment.

> 'It was you, it was you, I know it,
> You were the one for me,
> you were my destiny
> and you always have been.
> But one day I found out
> that I wasn't your destiny
> and my heart was broken. . .'

Romeo and Juliet lay lifeless on the ground. Megan's voice grew faint as she reached the last line of the final chorus. She strummed her guitar one last time and lowered her head, her eyes full of tears. There was silence.

Moments later, the audience were on their feet, clapping, cheering and whistling. Their applause almost knocked the cast off their feet as they lined up for their bows.

I did it! Alice thought in amazement. *I made my dreams come true!* Feeling faint with happiness, she scanned the crowd for her mother. *Can you see me, Mum? This is me, the real Alice!*

Mrs Barnes sat in the front row, clapping and beaming. The drama class had done the school proud. Meanwhile, Mr Bradford was telling his friends the theatre producers that Edward was a chip off the old block, 'just like his father and grandfather before him'.

Alice's mum couldn't take her eyes off her talented daughter. *She's a real actress*, she thought. *The real deal!*

From backstage, Amber watched Edward walk out to take the director's bow. He smiled with pleasure as the applause increased to almost deafening levels – he had no qualms about taking credit for the show. Amber was tempted to rush out there and push him off the stage. But then she decided that it really didn't matter who was being clapped or credited with the show's success. What was important was that *Rockspeare* was the biggest and best end-of-year show the school had ever seen. What mattered was the warm, fuzzy feeling she was having as she watched her school friends celebrating their triumph. It was the most amazing sense of achievement.

We did it! she thought.

Amid the party atmosphere backstage, Alice rushed over to Andrea. 'We owe Amber big time, don't you think?' she said. 'I was wrong to think she wasn't a real friend.'

'Do you have anything particular in mind?' Andrea asked.

Alice looked over at Thomas and back at Andrea, who giggled. 'Come on!' she said.

They ran at him, ambushed him and dragged him towards Amber.

'Anderson, you need to do something for us!'

'What's going on?' he asked.

'You need to talk to someone, that's what,' Alice said.

'Who?'

Suddenly he was face to face with Amber. She smiled hesitantly. 'You were brilliant, Thomas – the best Romeo ever.'

'Thanks, I...' His phone started beeping. 'That's

strange, I've never heard it make that sound before,' he said.

Amber snatched the phone out of his hands and threw it away. It landed halfway across the room and skidded along the floor. 'No!' he cried. 'I need it!' She grabbed his arm, but he shook her off. 'You don't understand. I have to get it back now!'

'Thomas!' she pleaded. 'Don't leave this time! You always run away.' She moved closer to him. 'You said we should talk and we didn't talk – but let's talk now. I like you.'

'There are things you don't know about . . . secrets,' he said. 'Things I don't even know. . .'

'I know that you're the perfect boy,' she said, with a hesitant smile. 'I know that you do really strange things, like vanishing. You know things you shouldn't know and you don't know things you should know. But right now I don't care. There's plenty of time for you to explain. I just want to know if you like me. So tell me!'

He looked into her eyes, asking silent questions. 'I like you, Amber. I like you a lot, but. . .'

'No buts, Anderson,' she murmured, reaching her hand out towards him.

He smiled and put his arms around her.

There was a hush as people noticed what was happening. Alice and Andrea watched wistfully, each of them remembering how they had once thought Thomas was their perfect boy. But, after everything that had happened, they felt glad for Amber that she was the one he had chosen. After all, Andrea and Alice had other boys on their minds.

Megan put on her headphones and walked away. She and Thomas – it wasn't meant to be and she was OK with that. She smiled sadly to herself and turned on her favourite track about love. Music was the best escape when you found yourself with nowhere else to hide.

'Amber and Thomas are together!' people were whispering backstage. 'This is going straight on Real Life.'

As Thomas held Amber in his arms, she felt like the fairy princess she had always secretly dreamed of being. Her whole world had changed. She had finally shrugged off every last trace of the old Amber, like a butterfly coming out of a cocoon.

Thomas gently moved away from her and looked deep into her eyes.

'Bye,' she said.

'I'm going to get my phone, OK? I'll be back,' he said.

No one noticed the momentary expression of pain on Edward's face as he watched Thomas and Amber, before he turned and started walking away. No one except James, who followed his friend as he made his way out of the theatre.

Alice rushed up to him. 'James! I'm here! We can talk now!' she said, smiling happily.

'Alice...' He turned and hugged her. 'I have to go after Edward,' he said. 'He needs me. I'm his only friend. You understand, right?'

She nodded. 'I miss you,' she said softly. 'I behaved like an idiot around you, I'm sorry. And now I was wondering if we're still together – if you still want to be?'

'We'll talk about it tomorrow, OK?' he said, hurriedly. 'I promise!' And he rushed off after Edward.

'Boys, huh?' Alice's mother said, from over her shoulder.

Alice whirled around. 'Mum!'

Her mother crossed her arms. 'Don't you "Mum" me!' she said, frowning. 'I'm furious with you – you lied to us again!'

'I'm so sorry,' Alice said, 'but—'

'You'd better be! But, just to make sure, I'm going to punish you with...' Alice winced, expecting to hear that she was grounded again. '...Double helpings of choco-cream cake,' her mother said, laughing. 'We're just waiting for your dad to get back and then we'll go and celebrate together!'

Alice threw her arms around her mum's neck. 'Did we win the volleyball?' she asked.

'Of course we did. We're the Keats family! We always win, even when we're not playing.'

Alice couldn't believe it. So everything had turned out for the best! Then she remembered her brother. 'What about Daniel?' she asked.

'He'll get over it, sooner or later, you'll see.'

'I hope so,' Alice said.

Andrea felt her cheeks heat up as she looked shyly at Jay. She tried to ignore the fact that Sara was standing next to him. Were they glued together? 'What an incredible show! We really liked it,' Jay was saying.

'You're really good at painting,' Sara added.

'Thanks,' Andrea said. 'I—'

'I wanted to tell you—' Jay interrupted.

'Yes?' she said eagerly.

'We're leaving for New York next week, so we must get together before then.'

'Oh, OK,' she said, trying not to show her dismay. She batted away her feelings of confusion and smiled as he and Sara walked away.

Bill was making an announcement. He was still wearing his top hat, still half in character, posturing and gesturing as Mercutio. 'Fair lovelies!' he declared when he saw Amber, Andrea and Alice. 'Mercutio himself – that's me! – has organized a party – the *Rockspeare* party! – at his humble house.' He took an exaggerated bow. 'And you're all invited!'

'Er, thanks, Bill,' they said, wondering how they could get out of it.

'Don't miss it – everyone will be there!' he warned.

'Um, I need to get ready first,' Alice said.

'Maybe later?' Andrea added.

Amber laughed. 'Much later,' she said.

'Whenever you wish, ladies,' he said, turning to join everyone else. 'Mercutio's house awaits.'

'OK!' they called after him, looking at each other with relief. 'Phew, that was a near miss!'

The three girls sat on the edge of the empty stage, staring into space. 'You know, I have to find a way of talking to James,' Alice said. 'I always get so tongue-tied.'

'And I have to find a way of winning Jay back,' Andrea said. 'He can't go on acting as if nothing's going on.'

'I just have to find a way to stop Thomas disappearing,' Amber said, 'although I know there's no point in trying!'

'He vanished again?' Andrea asked.

Amber rolled her eyes. 'Yeah.'

They paused to think about this – and the next moment they had collapsed into fits of laughter. Amber threw her head back and looked up at the roof of the theatre. 'It's been a crazy year!' she said. 'I started out barely knowing you – and I couldn't stand either of you. Then everything changed, after that detention, after Thomas and *Rockspeare*...'

'It's hard to believe, isn't it?' Alice said. 'You were the queen bee, I was the school clown and you, Andrea, had your head so stuck in your books that no one knew the real you.'

Andrea laughed. 'Even *I* didn't know the real me. I was so focused on my studies that I'd blocked out almost everything else. We've all changed. You were too scared to tell anyone about your love of acting, Alice. And, Amber, all you cared about was being popular.'

'I guess I got my confidence from being so-called popular,' Amber said. 'But it wasn't real confidence or real popularity. It didn't mean anything, as it turned out.'

'I didn't have any confidence at all!' Alice giggled.

'That's definitely changed!' Amber said. 'Things are so different after *Rockspeare*. It feels like I've discovered what's really important.'

'Me too. I've realized that there's more to life than

getting good grades,' Andrea said, 'and I'm finding it easier to talk about things. . .'

'Why have we changed so much?' Alice asked. 'Do you think it's all down to Thomas?'

'No!' Amber yelped. 'He's been nothing but trouble since the day we dreamed him up!'

'And still is,' Andrea added. 'Whoever he is!'

'Maybe that's the point?' Alice suggested. 'Maybe we would never have become friends without him?'

Amber jumped off the stage. 'We made friends *despite* Thomas, not because of him. I'd say that was an achievement in itself! Friendship rocks. Boys, grades and being popular are nothing compared to having really good friends.'

'It's just that we didn't realize it,' said Andrea.

'And now what?' Alice asked.

Amber smiled and raised her phone in the air. 'Now we take a photo!' she said.

Two minutes later, she posted a picture on Real Life – of three girls, arm in arm, the best of friends, for ever.